THE
VENETIAN
DAUGHTER

BOOKS BY ELLA CAREY

THE
VENETIAN
DAUGHTER

ELLA CAREY

bookouture

Published by Bookouture in 2024

An imprint of Storyfire Ltd.
Carmelite House
50 Victoria Embankment
London EC4Y 0DZ

www.bookouture.com

ISBN: 978-1-83525-679-4
eBook ISBN: 978-1-83525-678-7

For Fiona

CHAPTER 1

THE VILLA ROSA, TUSCANY, NOVEMBER 1943

A ceramic dish filled with olives sits atop the magnificent stone table where I sit. There is a platter of focaccia scattered with sea salt and rosemary, local cheese, honeycomb drizzling with liquid gold, a glass of limoncello, and the view. My dearest blue hills sit in the distance, soft and serene. The valley spreads out below the Villa Rosa, with its vines and olive groves, old stone farmhouses and medieval villages that have perched atop the far peaks forever, shadowy and romantic in the mist one day, golden in the sun the next, and yet, I am edgy. Something is about to break.

I toy with my glass of limoncello, my hands still glittering with the rings that my late husband, Arturo, gave me when we became engaged over twenty years ago. And all the time I'm sitting here, I'm waiting for that dreadful sound of a motorbike scooting up the driveway from the village at the bottom of the hill, for the sound of footsteps clipping on the gravel driveway, for the way people bow their heads when they bring news from the post office these days.

I twist my hand this way and that. If only it were to be my beloved late husband walking up the driveway toward me, a smile on his cheery face as he waves his hat to ward off the warm summer sun. Yes, in my dreams, it is summer. In my dreams, always I go back in time before the war, and it is when I sit out here at the day's end that I feel he is near. There is something about the breeze that does it, the way the lavender sways just so in the late afternoon, the way the sun glints on the summerhouse on the lowest terrace in the gardens, where Arturo used to paint.

It seems like an age ago that the Villa Rosa's garden resonated with the joyful voices of our children, Nico and Rafael, as they played hide-and-seek in the orchard in the terraced garden, Nico's cheeky blond head popping out from behind a tree, the sweep of Raf's long dark eyelashes curving on his cheeks as he looked down to show me a painting he made, and then later, my beautiful young men sitting in the sun, discussing parties, university.

I stand up, fingering my necklace, the Villa Rosa pink and glorious behind me, her windows shining out over the valley while she catches the last rays of the sun like a girl glorifying in her youth. But she and I have been through far too much together. We both know that the Tuscan sun doesn't only shine pure gold.

Standing has not helped soothe me at all. From here, I can see the spot in the rose garden where Arturo died in my arms after suffering a sudden heart attack when he was walking down to the village to chat with his friends. There is the curve in the driveway where I last glimpsed my eldest son, Nico, in 1940 before he left in anger over what he called my ridiculous politics, my lack of conviction that Il Duce's decision to align with Hitler was in the best interests of Italy, and now my eyes turn heartbreakingly toward the spot by the wrought-iron gates where my youngest son, Raf, tipped his cap at me in farewell before he left to fight in Hitler's war.

Oh, why can memories not be simple?

I close my eyes and take in a deep breath of cool air. When I open them again, the cypress trees that were planted in the aftermath of the Great War in remembrance of the young men who died between 1914 and 1918 look to be a darker, more forbidding shade of green than usual, and long shadows are falling over the valley, shading the hills and turning them indigo, navy, all shades of blue.

I turn away.

Agitated, I walk through the gauzy sheer curtains that shade the French doors into my study. It is almost time for the after-noon news.

My desk feels better with its crisp white documents and reminders of the businesswoman I have become since Arturo's death. I focus on the bills for repairs to farm equipment, neatly typed tables relating to quarterly crop yields, alphabetical lists of the farmers who are struggling for food, dates that we have sent supplies to assist their families due to the ongoing rationing and privations of war. Names of the wounded and dead tenants are updated weekly when any tragic information comes through.

My secretary and I have lost count of the days when I sent condolences or paid mourning families visits, sitting with grieving widows, and holding their hands. At least they know that I understand some of their suffering, that I have experi-enced a similar loss to theirs, but every time I sit in the kitchen of an old farmhouse, with its wood-fired stove, chairs scraping on neatly swept stone floors, herbs sitting on the windowsills and hanging from the ceiling along with the old blackened pots and pans, I feel that we humans have learned nothing since we lived in Europe in medieval times, battening down our villages, fortifying the hills with castles against invaders. This is the modern era, and yet fathers, brothers and adored sons are being sent away to battle at the whim of those in power, and the toll on the families in the valley is becoming too heavy to bear.

So, back to my desk. Work is such a relief in troubled times. My papers are all organized with great precision, everything pinned together in neat stacks with paper clips, and yet I can hardly distinguish one document from the other. I reach for a glass of water, only to place it back down again.

When it is time for the news bulletin, I go to the wireless, turning the round knob on the walnut panel to the right, clicking it into action, as if hoping that it will reassure me that everything is all right. But I know it won't. We have all begun to dread turning on the news, knowing we are likely to hear of yet more tragedy and loss, more worry for our boys away fighting. The last movement of Mozart's Symphony number 40 in G minor swells into the room.

I go to stand by the window. Hitler's war has been a disaster for Italy; we have endured Mussolini's reprehensible siding with the Nazis, sat at home while our government sent our boys off to the failed North African campaign, waited for the inevitable death tolls every day, then, after one moment of relief when we formed an armistice with the Allies while Mussolini was stood down this summer, crowds celebrating in the villages, and people waving the Italian flag, the Nazis marched into the north of the country and placed Mussolini back as a puppet leader again.

So, now, we northern Italians are living under the Germans in an "occupied territory," ruled from Germany by Hitler, while the Allies are moving up through the south. Meanwhile, the Germans tell us the British are raping and attacking our Italian girls and women on the way. Allied planes swoop overhead, targeting the northern cities, trying to beat the Nazis down, and refugees are attempting to escape to the south. Children, mothers, babies, the elderly, all caught up in this, arrive daily at the back door of the Villa Rosa, begging for food, their bellies distended, mothers unable to produce milk. The members of my household and I are out there in the mornings handing out breakfast to a new group of people every day. My gardener, Alphonso, bless him, is scattering enough vegetable seeds in the garden to feed every refugee that comes to the villa's back door.

I sit down on one of the silk-covered sofas in the middle of the room, draw a cigarette out from the pack on the coffee table, and light up. Smoke filters out into the loaded air as Mozart comes to a resounding close.

The introductory music for the news broadcast flares into the room, the gauze curtains flutter along with my insides, and the announcer begins in clipped, formal tones.

Arturo looks down at me from his portrait over the mantelpiece, his light brown hair combed neatly, his open, kindly round face with that dimpled smile. I sigh and wring my hands over and over, turning my rings like a rosary. *Watch over Nico and Raf. Keep them safe, my darling. For whatever reason, you were taken away from us far too young. But I believe you know what's going on. I believe that you would do all you could to protect them both. Please, God, keep them both safe, no matter what.*

Our boys, my boys. My heart.

I tap the cigarette in the ashtray and then the news broadcast begins, the announcer speaking in clipped, formal tones.

"*The Congress of Verona of the Italian Republican Fascist Party, in charge of the Italian Social Republic, also known as the Salò Republic—the fascist state set up in Northern Italy after the government signed an armistice with the Allies and fled to southern Italy—have met in Verona for the purpose of discerning a new direction for the country...*"

"Oh, for goodness' sake, get on with it," I snap, sounding like my British mother in Venice now. "We know our government is ridiculous, but must you labor the point?"

"*At the Congress, the new government has denounced the Italian monarchy.*"

There is a pause, perhaps for effect.

"*The Italian Republican Fascist party, directed by Hitler, has instead proclaimed the Social Republic supreme. The Social Republic supports the continuation of the war in order to defeat the Allies and to defend Italy's territorial gains.*"

Territorial gains? I cross my legs and stare at the chandelier.

And then he says it.

"*All members of the Jewish race have been declared foreigners in Italy. They are considered of enemy nationality and will be treated as such.*"

The announcer clears his throat.

I sit perfectly still. The curtains are still. My pulse is hard in my throat.

Jews will be treated as enemies.

Tears prick the backs of my eyelids, and I stand up. Shame for my country spreads through my trembling body, and I go to stand by the French doors again, pulling the curtains open, desperate to see the garden now. Alphonso is clearing away his gardening tools and I am reminded that this world, Tuscany, the villa and its gardens look like an idyllic world, but the dark feelings inside me warn me that everything has suddenly become much darker, much more bleak.

My oldest friend is Jewish. I love her like a sister. Talia is—*was*—a teacher in Venice until my father and I secured her and her father, a beloved doctor, passage out of Italy in September. It was heart-wrenching, saying goodbye, knowing that she may never be able to return home, wondering whether I would ever see her again. But there are so many Jewish citizens remaining in Italy. The Italian police did not enforce the exclusionist policies when the Nazis invaded. Clearly, the government are addressing that now.

The announcer's voice breaks into my thoughts. "*The Jews have enjoyed protection in Italy until now, but the Congress of Verona has declared today that all Jews will be arrested and deported to Germany with the help of the Italian Fascist police.*

The process is to begin immediately. Effective immediately." He coughs again and stutters a little on his repeated words.

I swallow a lump. I already miss Talia, so very much. The last time I saw her in Venice in September, we held each other for a long time. She and her father were headed to Palestine, and then to New York. They should both be there by now, safely. Of course I have not heard anything from them, but I am comforted by the thought that she will not become caught up in this latest round of terror, although my heart goes out to the countless Jewish people fleeing.

The house seems to echo around me. It feels empty—so empty. My sons both gone... no Arturo to support me, to rail against the madness of the world with me. And no Talia.

At least she is safe. On her way to safety.

I turn off the wireless and settle down at my desk, forcing myself to focus on my letters. Anything but the war. But war permeates every part of my life, my mind, body, soul.

I push aside these dark thoughts and focus, force myself to read my correspondence.

"*Signora? Scusa?*"

I jump like a scared cat at the sound of my secretary's voice, my eyes swiveling to where she is standing, long dark hair in its customary ponytail, neat red skirt, and blouse. In Cara's hand is a buff piece of paper. An address and a name typed in capital letters.

Mine.

Suddenly, my hands turn cold.

A telegram.

CHAPTER 2

No.

I stare at the telltale cream paper as if it is a death warrant. Telegrams usually are.

Tentatively, I take the thing I've been dreading all day from Cara's outstretched hand, turn it over, and slide my finger underneath the lip to open it up.

"Contessa? Can I get you anything? Water?" Cara asks.

"No, no, no." I am repeating myself. I know it. If I wasn't sitting down, I would collapse.

And then I scan the simple words, over and over again. Are my eyes playing tricks on me?

I bend forward, closer to the thing as if trying to make sense of it, shaking out the paper, one hand carving through my blond hair, tied in a chignon.

I never left Venice. Please, help me. T.

I do a double take, staring openly at it. Is it a trick? We saw Talia and Dr. Baruch leave with a trusted friend, who drove them to Ravenna, from whence they were supposed to stow away on a troop ship to Palestine. And from there, my father took great care to book them an urgent passage to New York. It was incredibly difficult to organize, but we said goodbye, my own tall, gray-haired papa kissing the short, owly Dr. Baruch on the cheek, me stifling tears as I held Talia close, not wanting to ever let her go before we hid them under the cover of darkness in the back of my wooden boat, *Mimi*, and I took them to our contact. This was before the Nazis invaded, and we planned it, because we knew that if we were invaded, we would be living under their curfews. And that time has come. So if my friends didn't leave...

"*Santa Maria...*" My voice cracks. I rub at my eyes, hopelessly trying to hide my tears from my secretary. *Jews are to be deported to Germany. Effective immediately.*

And Talia never left? Why?

"Contessa Evelina?" Cara's voice cuts in as if from far away.

My heart is thudding dully in my chest. "No," I whisper, helplessly. "Please, no, darling. Not now."

I tip my head back. Talia was always independent, but so was I, and this was what we loved about each other. We used to sit in the back of the classroom, not doing our schoolwork, infuriating our teachers. But what Talia taught me was that life was the most important thing. It was extraordinary when, years later, she turned around and became a teacher, devoting herself to her children. She never did anything by halves.

A yellow dress. The park around the corner. Water laps at the edges of the lawn and a girl my age, with long dark curls and pretty brown eyes, reaches up to open the playground gate. I let the swing slow, immediately drawn to her, her mischievous smile, pink cheeks, her mother's silk scarf blowing carelessly in the fall breeze. And the girl is running toward me and I'm already jigging up and down on my seat.

"*Buongiorno,*" I say, my eyes swiveling to my stern nanny on the park bench.

The girl in the yellow dress leaps into the swing next to me. I've never owned a yellow dress. "Let's swing as high as we can go and never stop," she laughs. "My name is Talia. Who are you?"

"Evie!" I shout, suddenly buoyed by her energy, buoyed by her joie de vivre.

She laughs, uproariously.

And it is as if my life begins then. We kick our legs and arch our backs and we are flying. Flying way above the ground. I am swept away with the swing and her giggle is infectious, a cackle that starts small and rises, like bubbles rising through a glass of pink lemonade. The sound of her joy feels so real and so powerful that I feel brave enough to ignore the warning on my nanny's face, the dint between her eyes, the fact she is packing up her knitting and coming toward us, shaking her head.

Nanny calls my name and warns me that I am going too high. I see the way she shakes her head, pats her rigid, steely gray hair, her voice scratchy and thin in the sunshine. But I swivel my head, and Talia grins at me and off we go. My little legs in their blue stockings stick straight out in front of me as we go up, up, and Talia's eyes light up even more. We fly as high as we can, my blond hair trailing behind me and her dark curls gorgeous in the wind.

A breeze flutters the papers on my desk.

Cara is closing the curtains over the French doors.

I stand up and stumble across the study. "Cara, I shall be going away for a little while. To Venice. Will you and Alphonso take care of things for me while I am gone?"

Cara pauses, her fingers on the heavy brocade curtains. "Sì, signora," she says quietly. "I do hope everything is all right."

Her eyes flash against mine a moment, and I hold my hand up as if to ward off the truth. "Of course," I say. "I..." My stomach clenches. "I have something I need to take care of."

I can't believe this. Where can I possibly start?

CHAPTER 3

I throw a suitcase on my bed and fling my wardrobe open, my stomach fluttering, pulling out clothes. It is November. So, Venice will be cold, chillier than Tuscany; misty mornings, a stillness over the lagoon. My mind racing, I reach for scarves and boots and cashmere sweaters and coats and woolen skirts.

A maid appears in my doorway, and I wave her off, assuring her that everything is under control. But my thoughts are spiraling. From 1938 until this September when the Nazis invaded Italy, Italian Jews were banned from their government jobs, stopped from marrying non-Jews, and forbidden to enter the armed forces, but Talia had gotten away with operating under the noses of the Italian Fascist police in Venice because they did not often enact the harsh laws, and because she was a respected teacher who taught many of the officials' children at the local state school. Goodness knows that teachers have been in short supply, and her children adored her. As does everyone who meets her. Not least me.

I fold a sweater and place it into the suitcase. With Talia, it's always as if she is keeping a beautiful secret, as if she's on the brink of telling you something wonderful. She told me when the

war started that she taught her classes how to dance the
Charleston as a way of easing their fears. Only Talia would do
something like this, especially as the Charleston is frowned
upon and considered degenerate by the Nazis. I can only
imagine the joy and escape for those little children.

I cross my arms, perusing my suitcase. She did mention that
many of the children she was teaching were orphans, did say
that it was going to be difficult to leave.

She never mentioned that the boat to Palestine was
missing one of its passengers. If she's not left Italy, she will
have stayed in Venice for the children. And what of her
father? He must have left presumably. Santa Maria. Oh, the
poor doctor will have endured that risky, dangerous journey all
on his own.

My mind drifts back to the 1920s. Red lipstick, bobbed hair,
drop-waisted silk dresses and high heels. Glorious whole days
wearing our pajamas and high heels on the beach, made desperately fashionable by Somerset Maughan's wife. Afternoons
lying around, watching the parade of American celebrities who
tripped their way to the Lido after stepping off the Orient
Express. Nights dancing to Cole Porter at the Hotel Excelsior,
mornings walking along the broad, shady avenues of the Lido,
eyeing the handsome guests, men falling in love with Talia left,
right and center. Her flirting, but never falling in love. It was me
who did that.

I shake my head. I don't have time to think about this.
Not now.

I clip my suitcase closed, slip my handbag over my arm, and
heave my luggage out of my bedroom.

Once I am downstairs and outside the front door beneath
the fan light that overlooks the front porch, Alphonso drops his
rake and rushes across, wiping his hands, and apologizing for
the dirt on them. He insists on carrying my suitcase, walks me
up to the garage behind the house, no questions asked.

"I suppose Cara has informed you that I shall be going away for a brief period," I tell him.

Alphonso places the suitcase down on the neatly raked gravel outside the garage and wipes a hand across his sweaty brow, the pink sunset catching on his graying hair. "Si, Contessa Evelina," he says.

He opens the garage, and there it is. My beautiful little Alfa Romeo 6C sitting waiting for me, red paint gleaming, jaunty headlights peeping out into the pink sunset. I sigh loudly. Thank goodness for small mercies.

I check the pocket of my coat for my *Kennkarte* in case I am stopped by the Nazis on the way. My fingers touch the stamped identification paper and recoil because in my own country, I have to prove my nationality, and because I have something to hide.

Alphonso glances around as if someone might be lurking in the driveway before he goes to the secret stash of gas that I have hidden in the back of the garage. He fills the tank and eyes me.

"Contessa Evelina," he says in his precise voice.

I raise a brow. "Yes?"

"It is not my place, Contessa, but I have to..." He coughs. "I must say that Count Arturo would be worried if he knew you were going out driving at this time of day. The Nazis are out on the roads in force. It's not safe. And especially not for a woman alone."

I sigh heavily, tapping my foot, fidgeting with my keys. "Yes," I say. "You are sweet to worry about me, but I shall be fine."

I'll drive to the island of Tronchetto and then take a gondola to my parents' palazzo on the Grand Canal. I shall stop in Ferrara for the night, then leave well before dawn to arrive in Venice at first light. I shall deal with the Nazis if they stop me. I shall tell them that my father is ill. My hands shake with trepidation, but I must keep any fears at bay.

When Alphonso has finished filling the gas tank, I slip into the leather seat, pull on my driving gloves and wrap my blond hair in a silk scarf.

"How long will you be gone, Contessa?"

My hand is poised. The key is in the ignition.

"For as short a time as possible," I say, quietly. "Goodbye, Alphonso. I have left instructions for Cara on my desk." I move to turn the key, then stop. "I know that you will take care of the gardens as if they are your own while I am gone. You know how much I appreciate this."

I feel his sad stare as I fire up the engine and pull out of the garage.

What I don't tell him is that I am not returning to the Villa Rosa without my friend.

Dawn is the time to come to Venice, and arriving in a gondola is best of all. The Doge's Palace is bathed in pink champagne, and the sky beyond Giudecca Island holds all the glorious colors of a pearly oyster shell. But the elegant lampposts whose orbs would usually glow golden in the frosty morning sit in darkness, like strange ghostly trees waiting until the war is over and they can be lit up again.

Like so many Venetians, I accepted without any surprise that Venice was one of the first cities that Hitler and the Allies placed on the list of treasures that must not be damaged throughout the war. I know that in many ways we are lucky, when other cities have been brutally attacked.

I glance at the palazzos that line the Grand Canal as I steer Mimi toward my family's home. There is something comforting about the old buildings, their windows not boarded like those in cities under threat.

Bathed in the pink sunrise, Venice is part gaudy old guest at a ball who must be respected, part immovable queen. The palazzos sit like grand old great-aunts who have stayed up far too late, tottering in pink dresses, their front doors opening straight out onto the canal with the water lapping up to their knees. Gondolas are moored outside the entrances, bobbing on the freezing deep green water as they have for centuries.

I navigate my little *Mimi* carefully along the canal, avoiding Venice's treacherous shallows as my father taught me long ago. As I move further away from St. Mark's Square, Venice wraps me deeper into her past, the great trading days of the Venetian Republic, her massive accumulation of wealth, leaving her with families like mine who are elite and aristocratic, untouchable. We were independent right up until Napoleon invaded and brought Venice's supremacy as a republic to an end. By then, her trading days were long gone anyway as the Portuguese and the Spanish had taken over, so in the eighteenth century, Venice transformed herself into a carnival, a circus, a freak of ingenuity and a show-stopping beauty all at once.

I finally turn in toward my family's palazzo that has stood in the same place since the sixteenth century, and I feel a sharp tweak of worry pinching my insides. I start at the sound of a bird taking flight from the jetty, and although my gaze remains focused on the section of the pier where I want to moor *Mimi*, I pray silently that I am not too late. If the Gestapo have been rounding up all remaining Italian Jews and transporting them immediately, what chance does a teacher have when everybody knows where she lives and works? While the police have treated Talia fairly, that is true, there would be elements of her community who would, tragically, be pleased to see her carted away. There are those who support the Nazis and who honestly believe their policies will create a stronger Europe.

I maneuver *Mimi* into place and reach down for my suitcase, taking my old brass key out of my handbag, and letting myself into my family's vast marble entrance hall. I stop and toy with a silver photo frame. My mother smiles out at the camera, her strawberry blond hair tied back into a smooth chignon, her slim frame adorned with a long golden evening gown, embellished with a huge bow on one hip, and her wide green eyes smiling at the camera. And next to her is my father, his arm proudly around my beautiful mother, the indent in his chin showing in his grin. They are living with rationing, yes, and they are treading around Nazi rules, but my parents still have their home and each other, unlike our Jewish population, for whom everything is gone.

I glance at the clock in the entrance hall: 7 a.m. I should put my suitcase in my old bedroom, turn around and go straight to Talia's house, but the elaborate pink, white and gold seventeenth-century painted friezes seem heightened and forbidding and the Murano glass and gold mirrors reflect my darting, blue-eyed gaze.

I finger my necklace and pick up my suitcase again. My relationship with my mother was at its strongest when my husband was alive. When I married Arturo Messina, I was not only the aristocratic daughter she had brought me up to be, but I was also the stunning girl who had landed herself a marriage into one of the most prominent families in Tuscany. The Messinas own forty-five farms and most of the villages in one of the most beautiful valleys in Italy, and Arturo's family were thick as thieves with Il Duce.

This also suited my mother, as Il Duce was himself thick as a thief with Hitler, and to her, just as to so many members of the British and European aristocracy, Hitler's plans to bring Germany back after the devastation of the Great War made sense. So, at dinner parties and at Venice's elegant cafés, my parents espoused the sensible nature of the tyrant who has sent us all to war. Since the Nazis showed their true faces, I don't know what they think.

But little did my mother realize how artistic and completely uninterested in prestige, power and politics my dear gentle and kind Arturo was. Little did she realize that he couldn't give two hoots as to whether someone drove a Ferrari or drank the best champagne.

When Arturo died, and I went into mourning. I grieved for him, and my mother mourned as deeply as I did. But now I am unmarried and certainly not the person to be running the entire Messina family estates, having turned away countless uncles and male cousins who insisted on taking over Arturo's enterprises after he died; the rental properties in Florence, the farms, not to mention the grape and olive growing estate. But then, the war started and the male relatives in both my family and the Messina family all had to go off and fight. So, I learned how to run the businesses and keep everything afloat.

I know I'm on borrowed time.

Every time I come to Venice, my mother reminds me that I am expected to marry again, and to marry well. To find a husband who will take over Arturo's family estates, as it is unseemly that all has been left to me. Every time I see her, she makes cutting comments that are designed to undermine the work I'm carrying out in Tuscany.

It is the way it is, and yet, despite my grief over losing Arturo so young, I have found fulfillment and a measure of enjoyment in running the legacy he left for me. I am grateful to him for the beautiful home that is now mine, for the people from the village and the business acquaintances with whom I work, and for the fact that it feels like Arturo's spirit lingers over the Villa Rosa and is watching over me.

I stop at the entrance to one of the grand sitting rooms. This is where I will turn right into the family wing of the palazzo. Hoping to remain undetected, I carry my suitcase into Papa's sitting room. The green velvet sofa is in delightful disarray. Pink and golden cushions are scattered on the floor, and the silk bolster where my father likes to lie and read at night is placed exactly where he puts his head. There is a dent in it in the shape of a large egg. Several books are lying on the ancient pink and green Turkish rug, and the magnificent black wrought-iron light that Arturo designed as a birthday gift for my father, decorated with trailing grapevines and roses, hangs above it all. A single candle in a silver candelabra sits on the coffee table, worn down almost to the quick.

I pass by the magnificent tapestry on the wall, with its blue trees and images of a long-ago shimmering Venice, throw open the double doors that lead directly from room to room and make my way upstairs to the family's bedroom wing.

As I pass all the familiar things in the house—the silver-framed photographs of my grandparents, captured in moments long gone, picnics in secret coves around Positano, my grandmother's famous watermelon and mint punch, Palermitan aubergine involtini with pine nuts and raisins and parmesan cheese, my grandfather insisting on carrying the picnic basket for my grandmother and refusing my father's offer of help, parasols and swimming and strawberry tiramisu—I am reassured that I belong here, that this is still my home, no matter what my parents may think about the current war. But right now I have somewhere else I need to be.

I shall freshen up and slip straight out to Talia's house. *Mimi* and I know our way around the small canals that are etched into the fabric of Venice as well as a pair of crafty cats. All I hope is that I can find Talia quickly and take her back to the safety of the Villa Rosa.

As I step out and the crisp air hits me, and then unlock the front door of the palazzo and step inside the entrance hall of my parent's home, making my way upstairs, I'm thrown back in time.

It's a misty winter afternoon, cashmere coat, fleece-lined leather gloves, flared trousers, split so they look like a skirt.

Venice is decorated for Christmas. Darkness is falling and the smell of roasting chestnuts wafts through the chilly canals, lingering above the water, hovering like a miasma in the cobbled, silent lanes. There is a stillness in Venice that is magical. If you close your eyes, you can sense angels singing Vivaldi under the golden mosaic domes of San Marco, you can feel the presence of Carnevale's past, masks glinting in the craftsmen's stores with the promise of our great annual festival at winter's end.

It is the December I turn eighteen. *Mimi* and I pass through the tiny canals and as we carefully navigate our way through the deepest and safest water in Venice, my hands steer her wooden steering wheel instinctively, because I know this city, I know its aged beauty, I know it because it is my home.

Christmas lights twinkle through the windows and throw firefly patterns onto the still water. *Mimi* glides beneath me, specially designed to fit in the canals. The night is ours and we will be a party of three—me, *Mimi*, Talia. A magical circle that reality cannot break. It is as if the gorgeous wooden boat is calling to us, *Come and live your life with me. It is all an adventure. It is waiting, I am waiting, you are free—*

"Evie? What on earth are you doing here at this hour?"

I stop halfway up the hall in the family bedroom wing.

My papa's navy-blue silk dressing gown is wrapped around his dramatically reduced waistline and his thick gray hair is already neatly combed, even though it is early, even though he has not breakfasted yet. He surveys me, his blue eyes narrowing, until he opens his arms, and I move toward him, leaning into his lemon cologne and cigars. "I'm delighted to see you, but why did you not let us know?"

I lift my chin and pull back from his embrace. My own China-blue eyes meet his.

He searches my face as if seeking reassurance it is really me. "Do tell me you have come home for the duration, *Cara Mia.*

Every night, your mother and I have the same conversation. It is too isolated at the villa. We worry about you."

This is going to be a delicate explanation. I tuck my arm beneath my father's elbow and steer him further down the long echoing hallway, well out of earshot of my sleeping mother's bedroom. The sun throws patterns onto the old rugs through an arched window of stained Murano glass that looks over the garden and we stop at the top of the ornate stairs.

I remember how this part of the house was bustling with servants once, how extended family members would come to stay with us, along with British friends of my mother, on their grand European tours.

A foghorn blares out a mournful, long-lost note.

Papa glances toward my sleeping mother's room and reaches for the handle. "She'll be delighted to see you."

But I press my lips together tightly and take hold of his hand, leading him back down to his sitting room where we can talk in private. I swallow hard.

Papa's eyes search my face for a moment once we are in his sitting room, his mouth works, as if he is about to utter something, but then he stops. He reaches up and pulls off his glasses, wiping his eyes, and for a horrible moment I am worried he is going to cry. "Please, tell me you have come home, *bambino*."

I rub my hands against the soft wool of my skirt. This is already becoming complicated.

Do I trust my father? *Yes.* Do I like my parents' politics? *No.* But he has always respected and admired Talia's family, and long was a patient of her father's, Dr. Baruch. In a split second, I decide.

I may need to hide Talia here for a night. I need to ensure he is comfortable with the idea.

Oh, Talia, I do love you, but why did you not leave when we worked so hard to get you out?

"Talia remains in Venice. She never left. I have come to take her home. I may need your help, Papa."

Papa folds his arms. His narrow face is pinched, and he leans against the drink's cabinet, his foot tapping on the ground. "Not after we went to all that trouble to get her out. You are certain?"

I nod.

"I was prepared to help before the Nazis took over. Now? No. And you must not take any risks."

I focus my gaze out the window to the water in an attempt to keep a cool head.

"How could you think to put not only yourself but your mother at risk by even suggesting we become involved?"

I turn back to stare at him in exasperation, feeling my head shaking minutely from side to side. "It is hardly us who are at risk, Papa." My laugh is incredulous.

"Not true. Get someone else to do it. It's completely unfair of you to undertake something so dangerous, Evie. I trust this is the end of the conversation."

I understand my father's reservations, and his annoyance that Talia did not take up the passage he obtained for her to get to Palestine and then New York. But we have to face the reality as it is, and I, with my blond hair, my aristocratic heritage, and being female, the Nazis are less likely to question me than anyone else.

A foghorn sounds in the distance. My annoyance flares. It will be a German boat. The Allies cannot bring ships into dock anymore and the Nazis are in control of the inland waters, the land, the sea. It is difficult to get into the lagoon, almost impossible for Venetians to leave. The only Venetians who plow about in the lagoon that leads to the open sea are the local fishermen who have lived there for centuries. And Nazis.

"*Mimi* and I will take her." I say the words before I overthink this.

My father narrows his eyes. "This is not the 1920s, my dear."

"Oh, I'm well aware of that."

And just like that, I am thrown back in time. Midnight. *Mimi*'s navigation light throws circular, flickering golden patterns on the black water as we pull into the dock outside the palazzo. Lights flare from the front rooms out onto the canal, and my father walks down to us, his gaze fixed on me, his lips pressed into a narrow slash. Behind him trundles the always slightly befuddled-looking figure of Talia's father, Dr. Baruch, his bald head shining in the light of Papa's lantern as he tugs at his jacket, eyes on my elegant father, following Papa's indomitable lead.

Talia is wrapped in a cashmere blanket, my green patent leather high heels held in one hand. But I am clutching *Mimi*'s steering wheel, and my muscles are still jumping under my skin in revulsion.

At first, the man who approached me in the grand ballroom of the Hotel Excelsior on the Lido, where we danced every night in the summer until dawn, had only stood too close, spoken too softly in my ear. But when he followed me to the restroom, when he grabbed me by the elbow and tried to force me into the gilt elevator that led to the part of the hotel reserved for guests, I was struggling, and he had my arm pinned behind my back. When Talia appeared out of nowhere and hit him on the head with a glass, it smashed against the wall, and in the momentary panic, she grabbed my arm and we fled.

Talia and I ended up running down to *Mimi*, arms linked to get away from him, but as I steered *Mimi* out into the lagoon, I could see the young man's silhouette watching us in the lit-up entrance of the hotel. The thought of what might have been had Talia not been there left me shaken.

Talia and I share one last glance before our fathers descend on us.

"Are you all right?" she asks me softly.

"Thanks to you, yes."

She stands up and pulls me into a quick hug, enveloping me in the warmth of the blanket she has wrapped around herself. When she pulls away, she keeps hold of my shaking hand.

A lantern, my father's face. Dr. Baruch, close behind. And then, the scene fades. Back then, I thought that was the worst we would ever face. I wish I'd been right.

"You don't understand what the Nazis are capable of. What they *will* do to you," Papa says.

My father's hands move to rest atop the brandy decanter. He pulls out the stopper, pours a glass of liquid amber, his movements precise.

I wince. Brandy before breakfast.

Papa downs one glass and pours another. "She made her choice after all we did to help. I won't entertain any more discussion on it."

"You remember that night at the Excelsior."

"Yes." He strings out the vowel like a snake.

"You told me she may have saved my life."

Arturo's funeral. Early fall, deep red leaves, orange sun. Bursting vines, heads bowed down. Next to me Talia held my hand as she'd done since the day he died, when she dropped everything. Rushed to Tuscany on the earliest train, flew in the front door and drew me into her arms, sat with me in the summerhouse until I was all cried out, took my boys for a walk in the orchard when all I could do was curl up in a ball.

"I'm not here to ask you whether I should take care of her," I say. "I'm here to tell you I'm going to. I'm sorry you don't feel you want to help, but frankly—"

My father stares at me. "I know you're going to do it, darling. I just think that you have no hope."

I pull my leather gloves on. "And I have more faith in myself than that."

CHAPTER 4

My leather-clad hands sit steady on the wooden wheel. I steer *Mimi* through the canals that line Venice's districts, la Serenissima's *sestieri,* to Cannaregio, the old Jewish quarter, whose beating heart is being torn apart. I approach the Ponte delle Guglie, the old bridge of spires that has been here since the seventeenth century. A twinge of nostalgia pierces me because Talia and I used to stop here on our way home from school. This was our parting point.

I carefully navigate *Mimi* under the curved bridge, my green coat wrapped neatly around my frame, my makeup retouched in the bathroom to perfection after the altercation with my father an hour ago, exquisite perfume on my wrist, high heels encasing my feet, and a flutter of loose pebbles dancing around my insides.

A sharp breeze has picked up and there are no children out running and playing in the Jewish quarter, no cheerful sounds coming from the Jewish school. I risk a glance as I pass by the square, at the school where Talia used to teach until it was closed down earlier this year. It is locked and barred now. I swallow.

Mimi and I glide past a boarded-up synagogue on the narrow canal, the Star of David next to the swastika slashed in red paint across its façade.

The unease in my stomach swells and tightens, the deeper *Mimi* and I move into the district that has been the home of Venice's Jewish families for hundreds of years. It is as if a sweeper has come through and pushed everything away, children, the elderly, all gone.

I pass shops tainted with swastikas, *"Jüdisch"* written over their once proud signs—the kosher butcher, the fruit and vegetable purveyor, and the cake shop where Talia and I used to stop for afternoon tea treats. I remember the owner, and his wife who used to give us her famous apple cakes for free because Talia was Dr. Baruch's daughter and he had looked after the owner with great care when he was ill, coming to visit regularly, sitting by his bed, and reassuring him with the magical touch of his kindly hand.

Heaven knows that Dr. Baruch looked after everyone in this *sestiere*.

But now it is empty. Only the ghosts of the community hang sadly in the quiet mist, and only the odd sound of Nazi jackboots breaks the stillness in the air.

As I move through the narrow canals decorated with humpback bridges, I remember and can almost hear the Jewish women leaning out of their windows over the canal and chatting with each other over the water, about how well their babies were feeding, whether the matzo ball soup had turned out properly, where they were buying this summer's prettiest fabrics.

Talia's mother made beautiful clothes.

My heart catches as I remember being back in Signora Baruch's sewing room, sunlight beaming through the windows, the wireless, "Rhapsody in Blue", "Ain't Misbehaving", while the signora hums along, and her sewing machine whirs in time, carefully fashioning dresses for her neighbors. As a child my one ambition was to have a polka-dot dress made by Signora Baruch when I turned eighteen.

She makes it for me, and it is by far and away my favorite present, tiny white dots on a silky pale blue fabric. I twirl in the oval mirror in her sewing room like a five-year-old in her first party dress.

That night, Talia and I go to a girlfriend's birthday celebrations and when we come home, Talia's mother is waiting up for us with supper. Signora Baruch is as intrigued by the gossip as we are and chats with us into the wee hours.

Now, back in the reality that confronts us all, the sun falls behind a bank of heavy gray clouds, and the water turns from deep blue to dark gray, reflecting the sky, always, always a mirror of what is going on above.

The stories are terrifying about the Jewish community. Nazis coming to your door in the early hours when they know you are asleep. Like thugs, they are upon you. And before you know it, you are ripped away from everything you've ever known. Your home, gone, your family shattered. You are starved, humiliated, thrown in the back of a truck.

My hands are clammy on the steering wheel, and I grip it, tight, my knuckles turning white. My legs feel dizzy, and I realize that I'm holding my breath as we come closer to Talia's house.

It is well known that there are those in our city who have lived their entire lives not going to St. Mark's Square. It has been said famously that many of Venice's citizens only shop at their own marketplace, and if something is out of stock in their quarter, then it is considered out of stock in the whole of Venice because they will not travel far to search elsewhere. But as we approach the nearest piazza to Talia's house, one thing is certain. No one will be shopping here. It is silent and empty. And it is as if the desolate canals in the Jewish quarter are crying too.

My nerves tingle as I pass by the old ghetto, where, for centuries, Jewish citizens of Venice were locked away at night, with a curfew and strict rules. A Nazi soldier stands outside the entrance to the first ghetto in the world, and I avoid making eye contact with him as I pass. I feel his gaze, scrutinizing me.

It is strange to think that it was Napoleon who freed our Jewish citizens from living separate lives in the ghetto, that a Corsican man full of ambition liberated our Jewish citizenry nearly one hundred and fifty years ago after centuries of living separate lives from the rest of us. Under the Venetian Republic before Napoleon invaded, the Jewish community in Venice had to not only live in the ghetto, but they were forced to wear a yellow hat or a yellow badge to distinguish themselves from the Christians. Only Jewish doctors were allowed to wear black hats because they were in high demand. I sigh as I think of Talia's father. At night before Napoleon invaded, the gates to the ghetto were locked, and it was a kind of prison.

But the Jews here established their synagogues and build their congregations. They came to Venice from all over Europe, Germany, Spain, Portugal. They built a cultural hub and interacted with other intellectual communities in Venice and in our city, they printed nearly one third of the Hebrew books that were produced in Europe.

A gust of wind throws lost papers around outside the locked and barred gate of the ghetto. Tears fall down my cheeks now, as I pass by the doctor's surgery, where Dr. Baruch was a beloved carer for so many during his long and distinguished career in medicine. The once blue-painted front door is boarded up with plywood and someone has painted on it, the Star of David again, and that word: *Jüdisch*. An old paper with the times he practiced flutters in the wind. It hangs on to the window as if wondering when he will come home. I wonder if Doctor Baruch will ever be able to come home. I only hope he is practicing in America, in New York.

I wipe wretched tears away. And then, I switch into a wider canal. The sun now beams back through the clouds, that soft, glorious lemon yellow that can send shafts of warmth into a winter's day.

I moor *Mimi* as near to Talia's house as I can. Silently, looking around, especially behind me, I walk stiffly toward the red house where she grew up. As I move toward the front entrance that used to be pretty with geraniums in the window boxes, my heart fills with the sound of Dr. Baruch's gramophone playing soft classical music as a counterpoint to Signora Baruch's penchant for the latest songs. I remember he introduced me to Brahms, sitting smoking his pipe in the study. I close my eyes a moment and remember the taste of him giving Talia and me our first try of apple sauce on dark rye bread, of her calling him *"Deus,"* because to her, the dear, owlish man was like a god.

The house was always filled with the scent of coffee, honey, and almond cookies, and orange cake fresh out of the oven. As well as being a talented seamstress, Talia's mother worked for Dr. Baruch, greeting the patients, and often giving out tips that were all her own.

I know I am trying to replace the ache, the worry about what I might find in the house by filling my mind with memories of happier times. But it feels like as good a way as any to cope with the darkness that has imbued Canareggio, the only way to make friends with the occasional beam of sunlight that is still trying to shine through the clouds of war.

I stop at the entrance to the red house. On the front door, a swastika is painted like a jagged crow. The paint gleams treacherously in the rays of the weak sun. I curl my hands into fists, burying them deep in my pockets, resisting the urge to use them to wipe the paint away. My heart swirls, and my stomach caves in. I am too late. The house is marked, and Talia has been taken.

Now what?

CHAPTER 5

The only sound to break the silence outside the Baruchs' home is the water lapping along the canal behind me. I shiver violently, and my white-cold hopelessness, the paralyzing shock, is replaced by glowing red anger. As I stand here, polarized in the strange light that is causing the water to reflect on the front of the house, boots play a snare drum beat on the cobblestones in the wintry air.

I swing around like a dancer in perfect time.

A single Nazi rounds the corner and comes to a stop in front of me, clicking his heels in the quiet. He raises his hand in that preposterous salute, shouting the words *"Heil Hitler"* that we are supposed to mimic.

I stand tall, and eye him, my lips sealed.

The Nazi appraises me, and his own lips sliver into a lecherous sneer that causes my blood to curdle in my veins. I jam my hands into my pockets, my hair lifting on the nape of my neck and rising to attention on my arms. If the man who tried to attack me at the Excelsior all those years ago gave me the creeps, this man is a thousand times worse.

I already hate the way he is looking at me, but he only steps closer, and places his face close to mine.

"*Kennkarte.*"

I pull out my identification papers. I have no choice.

"This house was saved for me by the commandant." He flips through my *Kennkarte.* "Signora Messina," he murmurs, his eyes lighting up with something I don't like. His requisite tightly clipped haircut, feathered so short it sits like fuzz on his head, frame icy blue eyes that are too close together, his nose perfectly aquiline. Cold eyes, cold heart. And he gets to live in Talia's family home?

My leg muscles tighten. My body wants to run, but I hold my ground.

"The commandant has particularly kept this house for *me.*" He repeats his reprehensible contention, folds his arms, and surveys the Baruchs' house. A satisfied glint lights his cruel eyes. "I shall be extremely comfortable indeed." He hands back my *Kennkarte.* "Visiting someone, Signora Messina?"

"Of course not," I say. My chest shudders and hurts as I breathe, but I refuse to look down, or away. To do so would be to admit defeat. It is bad enough having to pretend to be someone I am not, to dismiss Talia and her family.

"The inhabitants have been removed in accordance with the new government directives. You must move on. Go home. Immediately! For a woman like you, it is not safe here. There are still reprehensibles in this *sestiere.*"

Indeed, there are.

The Nazi clicks his heels together and waves me away.

I hurry off up the canal, my legs stiff, my knees wanting to lock. I gasp, expelling my breath as I pass by the neighboring houses, all marked with swastikas, slashed across front doors.

I remember Talia's neighbors dropping in for chats with Signora Baruch. They were the family's friends. And now, goodness knows, I will be a good friend. I swallow down tears, but I will not walk away from here without doing everything I can to get into the house. I don't care if the Nazis have already been there. I need to know whether she is truly gone, or whether there is some hint as to where I might find her.

A candle lights in my heart because there is another narrow canal that runs behind the house. I know exactly which of the gates that run along it leads to her back garden.

I walk around the block, picking up my pace. When I am exactly halfway down the lane that runs behind her home, I prize a loose brick out from Talia's garden wall, my memory guiding me quickly to the correct stone.

A flash of silver and brass graces my palm, and I close my fingers tightly for a second. "Perfect," I whisper, clutching at the key that opens the back gate and the back door to the house.

I take the silver key and insert it into the lock to the gate. It works like a dream, and I step into my childhood memories. The soft green lawn is still the same, and the trees and shrubs are carrying the last vestiges of beauty, leaves of muted gold and burnt orange drip from the branches as if singing the final song of fall. I close the gate that is set into the wall behind me and check it is secure. In front of me, the house sits, the back windows looking sadly out over the autumnal garden, and it is as if Talia's home, too, is grieving along with the weeping golden leaves on the trees. The air swells with sadness, moving like a miasma, and I have that strange feeling again that ghosts are around.

The back door leads straight into the Baruchs' kitchen. It is neat as a pin, but the feeling of emptiness in here is astounding, and I have to pause and lean against the scrubbed kitchen table and gather my breath before I pass into the long hallway that leads to the front rooms of the house.

My feet are soft on the Turkish rugs as the grandfather clock ticks. Nothing has been touched, and there is no evidence of a struggle. The paintings are still on the walls and a green umbrella leans against the wall by the front door. There are Talia's velvet pink slippers, a pair of her lace-up brown shoes. I flick on a light switch and the chandelier glows gold over the entrance hall. A blue woolen scarf is hanging over the banister.

I peer into the sitting room, the dining room, Talia's father's study where he used to sit with his pipe. The curtains are drawn. Nothing has been disturbed. The sense of order feels more sinister than if the house had been ransacked.

It is when I am halfway up the stairs that I hear a whimper coming from downstairs, at the back of the house. A shuffling, another cry, louder this time. I stand and freeze. *Talia?*

I turn back around. The sound came from downstairs, out the back of the house. My childhood memories are coming thick and clear, games of hide-and-seek, and I almost want to chuckle. Now, I am moving fast, knowing where I am going, knowing where I need to look.

Summertime. School holidays, hot sun, cool house. We'd tired of our paper dolls and wanted adventure. Hide-and-seek. I scared Talia by jumping out of the laundry chute.

Please, let her be hiding there now.

CHAPTER 6

The door to the laundry is wooden and like a farmhouse door, painted white, heading straight from the silent kitchen. It leads to a room that once smelled of freshly laundered linen, where the Baruchs' housekeeper toiled even on the hottest, most stinking of Venice summer days, when the canals were putrid and the air stifling. I remember one baking day in August, the poor woman was ironing, but would not take a break. Talia's mother plied her with glasses of water with sliced lemon drifting in the glass. There is a stoicism about Venetians.

I turn the door handle. Sheets are folded on the shelves that line the walls; the iron stacked neatly on the table in the middle of the room. And then I hear it again. A shuffling. I go to the hatch at the bottom of the laundry chute. Open it without hesitation. Is she here?

I am face to face with a little boy. My hand flits to my mouth, and for one wild moment, I am staring at the memory of my boys. The child's face morphs in front of my eyes. Nico, his green eyes alight with mischief, blond hair smooth as silk, always so inquisitive and chatty, wanting to know everything. And darling Raf, his dark curls in disarray, his huge brown eyes looking up at me trustingly, those eyelashes that swept across his cheeks. How I miss them.

I swallow back the tears that threaten to fall like a sheet down my face. The boy morphs back into himself and the memories of my little children float away on the wind. This child has light brown curls and brown eyes like dinner plates.

"*Buongiorno,*" I whisper.

The child looks at me but says nothing. He is perhaps six years old. His cheeks are pale, and his hands are shaking. "Are you German?" he asks.

I crouch down, moving to his level, but he folds his thin arms around himself. His wrists are too thin and the skin on his hands appears almost translucent.

"No, *bambino,* I am Italian, and a friend of Signoria Talia."

"She told me to hide." The boy regards me.

I hold out my hand, keeping it still in mid-air, too tentative to touch his shoulder, or grasp his hand. We stay like that, until, finally, he steps out tentatively into the room, and as I watch him, I am assailed by the heartbreaking argument that I had with Nico three years ago. After he left, the Villa Rosa ached with the same sadness that blew softly through Talia's trees. But here, here is another little boy who stands in front of me, beads of sweat on his upper lip and forehead, his curls sticking up wildly, and yet his head held high. And I can help him. I can help him now, even though I could not help my own son.

"Darling, where is the signora, Talia?"

I want to hug him, my eyes are filling up with tears, and I'm holding my breath, lest I rush out too many words and frighten him away, poor child. Imagine what he's already been through. I hate to think where his parents might be.

He blinks rapidly. "Signora Talia told me to hide here. I don't know where she has gone."

My lips start trembling. She knew the best hiding place, bless her, and she told him. "Did the Germans come to the house and...?" *Take her away...* I can't bear to ask my own question.

"There were Germans here," he whispers. And then his mouth starts working and his chest heaves up and down alarmingly. "Where is my teacher? Please?"

I want to collapse on the floor, curl up and cry. I need to hold something, grip something. Hold on for dear life to something real. So, I reach out and take the child's hand, my eyes darting about the room, and I search hopelessly for any sign that Talia might be here. That she might step out in one of the bright dresses she favored, a lovely scarf around her shoulders, that pearly smile of hers lighting up her face, bringing me home.

Touchingly, the child does not resist my grasp. He looks up at me, his chocolate eyes searching my face and looking a little puzzled, as if he can't work out why I am almost crying instead of him.

"I did what Signora told me to do. I buried myself in the laundry chute," he says, making it sound almost like an explanation.

I nod, my teeth biting down onto my bottom lip, my heartbeat racing. *Where is she? What on earth has happened to her?* "And did Signora Talia say she would return for you?" I can't help it, my voice sounds watery on the last word.

But the boy doesn't seem to notice. "The signora said my parents would come to get me and told me to hide. But they did not come. I blocked my ears because it was too loud when the Germans came, and I tried to sing a song in my head instead. My parents never came, but the Nazis did. I know because Signorina told me to watch out for it. She told me if I heard German, I must curl up like a ball. So that's what I did?" His voice rises with the last sentence. "I heard you calling the signora, and I cried. Sorry." He shakes his head. "I am hungry." He looks up at me, his upper lip curling, his face dejected.

My heart swells.

"What is your name?" I ask. "And, sweetheart, you have done nothing wrong. Not a thing." I am surprised by the calmness of my tone.

I should have come sooner. I should have known. How could I have known? Oh, Talia, what have you done?

I crouch down to get closer to the little boy. The look of dejection on his face clears momentarily, only to return, tenfold. "Mario. My name is Mario Di Maggio." He bites his lip and looks away.

"And Signora Talia told you to wait for your parents? You think they should have come by now?"

The child nods, and the house sits quietly behind us.

I wait a beat and then press my hand to little Mario's and, together, we make our way out the back door into the sadness of the garden. I have no plan as yet, but with this child's hand in my own, I feel more confident, an acute sense that I will not only save Talia, but that I will take care of her little student as well.

As we approach *Mimi*, I sweep the boy up into my arms, and carry him down toward my wooden boat, where I hide him under a blanket and tell him to stay quiet.

His face is ashen when I cover it over with a blanket, but just before I start the engine, a small hand appears from under the blanket. And I squeeze it, and I feel his warmth, his life.

All I can hope is that he will somehow lead me to find my friend.

When I arrive back at the palazzo, I bundle Mario up in the blanket and carry him inside. He tucks his head into my shoulder as we enter the back gate of my parents' palazzo. I move through the house, avoiding the rooms where my parents live, making my way like a shadow through my own family home.

It is only when we are safely inside my suite of rooms that I place Mario down. His little legs wobble and he hovers back and forth like a balloon floating in the breeze, before I lean down and whisper, "You must stay very quiet here. I shall go down to the kitchens and get you some milk, warm bread, and honey. And then, you can have a bath. Would you like to sleep after that?"

Mario nods, and, instinctively, I reach out and wipe gently at the trail of dried tears down his soft cheek.

Once Mario is safely tucked up in my bed, I go to find my parents.

My mother and father are sitting out on the balcony of the morning room, framed by the magnificent, timeless vista of the Grand Canal. In the warmer months, wisteria drips pearls of blue from the top of the balcony, lending its striking beauty to the soft domes of the Santa Maria della Salute church on the other side of the canal. The domes hover and shimmer above the water, placed gently to remind us all that true beauty does exist.

My father is enjoying a cup of black-market coffee. He is behind the newspaper he's reading, spread open wide, and I slip into the seat opposite him at the stone table. My mother, dressed in a pale pink cashmere ensemble, her green, catlike eyes made up, looks me up and down.

"*Buongiorno*, Evelina," she says. "You must have made a spur-of-the-moment trip. Is everything quite all right? Have you heard anything from Nico?"

"No," I say, looking down, feeling her eyes upon me. "Nothing."

"Well, you should write to him."

"I have. Again and again."

"It is getting ridiculous. What has it been? Three years? I

don't know, Evelina. He writes to me regularly. You know he is in Milano now?"

The fact that my son was not eligible for the army due to his short-sightedness was a sore point for him when Italy joined the war. I think there was an element of anger within him that he unleashed on me. But I am not going to take this up with my mother. Unfortunately, she has a habit of thinking in two straight lines. Clearly, the blame for what has happened with Nico lies with me.

Again, she looks me up and down, and I feel that old tightening in my chest that comes upon me when I am around her. Sometimes, it is difficult for me to breathe.

My father shakes his paper out and regards me over his reading glasses. "Help yourself to coffee, Evie. Tell us about the Villa Rosa."

"You are still running the entire place on your own?" my mother asks.

"It is a pleasure doing so. A distraction, I'm sure you'll understand. Unfortunately, most of my work these days is supporting widows and distraught mothers in the valley." I shake my head. "I'm afraid bad news is coming in almost daily."

My mother sighs, and my father reaches out and places his hand atop mine.

I pour myself a cup of real coffee, sipping it appreciatively, tipping my head back and closing my eyes. I have taken to drinking ersatz coffee like everyone else, but my father has a string of contacts. He goes to the Café Florian every morning with his old friends, where they discuss all the matters of the day. Minute, large, everything is dissected, heads shaken over the way the world is changing. I think there has been a softening in his political opinions since September, when he stepped in to help Talia and her father leave Italy.

Before that, he was such a supporter of Hitler. He and my mother have German friends who would come to stay and complain of the dire situation the country was left in after the Great War. When Hitler came and promised to make Germany strong and powerful again, my parents saw this as an opportunity to rebuild not only their country, but to strengthen the entire region. And when Mussolini aligned with Hitler, they thought that this strength made sense.

I remember my history teacher always telling us that in times of great struggle, a country will turn to a strong leader. But, in recent months, we have seen the slow but inevitable unfurling of Hitler's real intentions, to annihilate the Jews. My father had grown up in a city with a large Jewish population, and among his close friends, he counts Jewish businessmen. When the Nazis invaded, he arranged not only for Talia and her father to leave Venice, but two of his close friends as well.

I think the lack of control that the Nazi occupation affords the elite in this city has left them with a sense that they cannot do anything but play the game for now. Some of the wealthy citizens of Venice have gone out to their villas in the country, but my mother does not like the isolation of that old country house. Therefore, my father agreed reluctantly to stay in Venice with her.

"Your father told me that Talia was still here."

I flash a glance toward my father. My neck stiffens, and I push back my chair and stand up. I go and lean heavily against the balcony. "She was not at home."

My father shuffles his paper behind me. "Then there is nothing to be done."

"I cannot do nothing." The words grind out of my mouth. But I am sick of my parents living in this bubble of safety. Protecting themselves. Are they not seeing the quiet devastation outside the walls of the palazzo?

"You must not get involved," my mother says, her tone crisp.

I pause. Sigh. I know my parents can be difficult, but I also know that they would never betray Talia, and perhaps, if I can convince them of the danger that faces her, they might just agree to help. "There was a child, alone in the Baruchs' house."

My parents are silent.

"Santa Maria," my mother murmurs finally. "Well, what a mess this is. Why would Talia leave a child alone in her house?"

I turn around slowly to face them, my eyes adjusting away from the lovely mirage over the other side of the canal.

My father's blue eyes are darted toward my mother. He is rubbing her shoulder. "My darling, we know the answer to that."

She shakes her head. "So, there is a Jewish child in your bedroom, Evelina, I presume?"

I remain silent, letting them take this as they will.

My mother's painted lips widen in a cold smile that does not reach her eyes. She pats her still strawberry blond hair and taps her manicured fingers on the table. "You could have asked."

I do not dignify my mother's comment with a response.

"I shall find Talia as soon as possible and take them both to Tuscany."

She rolls her eyes and folds her arms. "How old is the child?"

"He is a little boy called Mario. I suspect he is around six years old. He is one of Talia students, and while I have not questioned him, clearly his parents have been... deported, and she must have been looking after him. The house was immaculate," I continue. "But the little boy told me that the Germans had been. Talia was nowhere in sight."

My mother tips her head back. "I told you not to get involved in this. It is true that you helped the Baruchs get out of Italy. Why on earth did Talia not take advantage of your kindness then?"

My father sends my mother a kindly look. "I know," he murmurs softly.

I pull out my chair and sit down. "There is no point going over that now. I was surprised myself that Talia had stayed here. But I suspect she did not want to leave students who may be orphaned."

My mother has the grace to redden. She places her hands on the decorated arms of the wooden chair, pushes herself back and sighs. "I suppose I shall have to go and meet this child. He can stay with us until you find Talia..." She lowers her voice. "But, Evelina, that is incredibly unlikely."

I bow my head. "I know," I say.

My mother stands up, adjusts her pink twinset, and leaves me alone with Papa.

He tents his hands and regards me. "Evie—"

But then, I gasp. Incredulously, I stare at the front page of the newspaper, as if I am in a daze. I peer closely. Closer again. My thoughts are fuzzy and yet my eyes are telling me with the greatest clarity that what I can see is real. But it cannot be. I want to stand up, walk away, anything but sit here staring at the photograph on the front page of the daily newspaper. I grip the unrelenting, cold stone table with both my hands until my knuckles turn white.

"*Santa Maria,*" I murmur, unable to keep my shock to myself. I must be mistaken. I must be going mad. Too much has happened today. I am seeing things. It cannot be.

I turn away from the newspaper for a moment, let my eyes rest on the serene scene beyond. Sky, the water spread out below, and the church. And then I look back and I am not imagining things.

Jack Sabo. I fell in love during those years at the Lido, it is true, but I let go, and I never thought I would see him again. But there he is, on the front page of the newspaper. Smiling. Handsome. Only faint streaks of gray at his temples give any hint that he has aged at all. Otherwise, he is exactly the same. And he is in Venice. Shaking hands with a Nazi.

. . .

Summer, 1920. The grand ballroom of the Hotel Excelsior. One of the most fashionable hotels in Europe, a playground for the rich and famous and the place to be from June to September for the smart younger set. Every morning, we wake up at noon, put on our silk pajamas and dressing gowns which we wear all day, and go out through the airy entrance hall to the terrace and then down to the beach.

Each guest has a bathing hut on the beach below the majestic set of steps that lead down from the hotel, and the more fashionable you are, the closer your hut is to the beach, the more beautiful your silk pajamas, the more elaborate your bathing costume.

We spend our mornings eating figs and melons and gossiping about the dancing the previous night. Every now and then, we step down to the Adriatic to swim, attendants with towels and beach carpets on hand.

All afternoon, we've been lounging beneath the magnificent façade of the Moorish building that overlooks the Lido, tanning our legs on the elegant day beds that are lined up exclusively for the use of hotel guests by their huts and sipping lemonade. If we want to, we can go to the tea dance in the late afternoon on the terrace, followed by pre-dinner cocktails before we go upstairs to change into evening dress.

That evening, an American girl—I hardly know who, but it doesn't matter—allowed us to change and shower in her suite. Pale-blue silk bed under a crowned canopy, soft-as-cashmere carpets, silken chairs overlooking the windows, open to the breeze and the balcony and the view. The water that feels like it could lap against the balcony is deep blue and feels so close that I could touch it, and this afternoon I went for my first swim of the summer in the sea.

I stand in the pale pink marble bathroom next to Talia. Her face is reflected in the mirror that is decorated with golden roses and leaves. A light breeze wafts through the half-closed shutters and we are both tweaking our lipstick, brushing our hair, twirling this way and that in our knee-length dresses, each of us wearing a few strands of my mother's pearls.

I pull a bottle of perfume from my purse and spray it in the air. Talia kicks up her heels, and walks into the scent, her navy-blue silk dress catching in the light, and asks me if I'm ready.

We go down to the terrace for dinner, giggling like schoolgirls, arm in arm.

Later, we are under the gleaming chandeliers in the ballroom, French doors thrown wide open to the private balconies, perfect for trysts. Arches run from one end of the room to the other, garlanded with deep green trailing ivy and scented with pale roses that are intertwined in the ivy leaves. More delicately colored roses sit in crystal vases on the tables, and a waiter is moving around the room lighting candles, another one is lighting the chandeliers.

Twilight is approaching and elegant waiters pass by the gorgeous guests, tanned from the sun. The waiters hold trays of champagne, deviled eggs, prawn cocktails, and slices of cucumber and cream cheese, as if to denote the magical hour before the ballroom is lit up and the dancing begins. We shall all dance up here, high above the twinkling lights that line the beach beneath the hotel. Much later, we will wander to the nightclub, Chez Vous, where cabaret performers will entertain us, and we will dance some more. Always, we dance, as if nothing matters and it never will again.

In the ballroom, Talia is whisked away to the dance floor by a handsome young boy we've met on the beach today.

The band strikes up Gershwin's 'Rhapsody in Blue'.

I slip down into a chair at the table that has been set for our party, made up of some old friends of ours from home and a set of bright young things from London, family friends I've known a long time. I arrange my dress, fan my hot cheeks with my free hand. I don't mind sitting for a while. The whole day has been a whir; a new group of young things from Cincinnati arrived today, wealthy, pretty, looking for new Italian friends.

I have friends here who summer at the Lido regularly, and my family will rent a suite later in the season, but at this point, who cares who is talking to whom. It's all a blur. As long as you are fashionable and young, you can dance with anyone, and chat with people from all over the world. It's as if we are all drunk on life, on living. On the fact that our lives have just begun. Every night we dance until dawn and then sleep until noon, and then come back the next day and do it all again.

I haven't been sitting for five minutes when he appears. Curved green eyes, strong jawline, light brown hair swept to one side, tanned skin, slow smile, a dimple on his right cheek. I watch him out of the corner of my eye as he slides into the chair opposite mine and lights up a cigarette, turning to watch the dancers, and then turning to me. His fingers are long and elegant, and he leans forward and taps his ash in the tray.

"Do you always sit down at tables uninvited?" I ask.

"Only when I want to," he replies. One of the Cincinnati boys. "And I've been wanting to for a few moments now." His green eyes look as if they are reading every inch of me.

"Well, I think you might've asked."

He sits back and crosses his legs, his cigarette draped elegantly in the fingers of one hand. "I can if it bothers you so much. Do you want me to move? Only, you see, I can watch you better from here."

My lips part to say something, but I sit back instead, stroking my arm idly, then toying with my long rope of pearls. "You mean you can *talk* to me."

"No, I mean I can watch you."

My senses are alive. He shouldn't be saying that, but he is, and he looks at me, unapologetically.

"I should go and dance with my friends." I stand up, but the man opposite me is standing too, and he comes around and takes hold of my arm.

"You forgot to tell me your name."

"You never asked."

"I'm asking now."

"Evelina."

"Lina," he murmurs. "It's a pretty name."

I start. No one has ever called me that. I scan the dance floor for Talia. See her. She catches my eye and raises her brow, staring at the handsome American next to me.

I extract my arm, but my hand catches against his, and knowing I'm reddening, I step away from him, my skin tingling.

"I'm Jack," he says, his easy smile running up and down my spine. "Jack Sabo. Nice to meet you, Lina. Dance with me," he says. "Dance with me, just once. If you don't like it, you don't have to do it ever again."

Papa lays the newspaper flat on the table and I stare at the photo. It's been twenty-three years, but I'm certain. It's Jack. My hands want to peel the paper from the table and stare and stare at it until I have an answer, but I cannot move.

It is Jack. Unmistakably. And he is shaking hands with a Nazi. In uniform. A swastika emblazoned upon the short man's arm. I think, if I am right, that the Nazi is the commander of Venice. I shudder. What foul play is this?

Did I never know Jack properly? Was I such a fool that I could fall in love with someone as reprehensible as this?

A sickening feeling swells in my stomach. What on earth is going on? And then my mind starts to run through worst-case scenarios. Talia was his *friend*. Did Jack know she was here, did he authorize her being taken away?

The problem is, no one is going to tell me where she is. This is how the Nazis operate; they come, they take people away, but they refuse to tell you whether they have them or not. I have heard of this happening in France, and I have no doubt it is happening here. People just disappear. There is no list of prisoners. There are only empty houses, and empty streets.

Tears of frustration prick the backs of my eyelids. I unbutton the top of my blouse, try to loosen the knot that seems to constrict my throat.

I reach across silently, pick up the newspaper, and show my father the front page.

Papa peruses the photograph, and then lifts his head slowly, and his eyes meet mine.

I read the first paragraph of the article out loud. "*Eminent American war correspondent Jack Sabo has returned to Italy to report on the glorification of the country under Hitler's rule. He will be sending daily wireless broadcasts back to the United States in Italian, to reassure the Italian-American population that their country is being well-managed, that everything is perfectly all right at home.*"

I stand up. I want to throw the paper into the canal. But I don't. I keep reading, sensing my father's gathering frown, the way his body is tensing.

My eyes race over the article. There is a paragraph setting out the fact that a contingency of Jewish Italians fled to America for the outbreak of war. And reassurance that those who remained in Italy would be interred according to the policies set out at the Verona Convention yesterday. There would be no exceptions. The city must be purged.

Jack Sabo, the article states in bold print, will tell the truth about "Hitler's generosity" to the millions of Americans who listen to his broadcasts. This will convince the United States that, even though we are at war with them, their concerns as far as Europe go are unfounded and that they should focus instead on the Pacific, if they must.

The Nazis have allowed certain journalists whom they trust and who are their friends to report back to their countries. They are proud that Mr. Sabo has taken up such a post. All is well and proceeding as it should be under the magnificence of the Third Reich here.

The paper falls by my side. I feel my cheeks burning, a sheen of sweat on my chin, my forehead. I'm disgusted, overwhelmed. My gaze moves to the last paragraph of the article which gives details of a reception for the press to be held at the Hotel Danieli this afternoon. Guests will be shown a short film that will form the basis of the news reports the Nazis expect to be sent around the world.

"I am going upstairs to ask Mother if I can borrow her red velvet dress."

Papa eyes me. "Keep out of it, please. There is nothing you can do about Jack Sabo. There is no need to make an appearance at the reception. And you cannot control or fix the fact that Talia never left. You should go back to Tuscany. I will ask around about this boy. Does he have a surname?"

"Di Maggio."

My father folds his arms. "And you, my darling, must protect yourself. Keep away from Jack Sabo, he caused you more than enough grief twenty years ago."

"I have to find out." The words come out from somewhere inside me, from some long-ago place that I thought I had buried. "And you know full well that I will turn this city upside down to find Talia."

My father sighs. "You have no idea what you are taking on."

I sit back down and survey the domes of Santa Maria della Salute through the bare wisteria's gnarled lens. It is as if the plant has created a web around the view.

I see the cold, too close eyes of the Nazi who followed me this morning. I see the swastikas painted on the boarded-up front door of my oldest friend's house. I see Jack shaking hands with those very people.

Did I ever know him at all?

CHAPTER 7

I adjust my mother's red velvet evening dress that she had trimmed, at the outset of war, from its original floor-length design to a shorter version to save fabric, turning the lower half of the dress into a little jacket. Diamonds glint at my ears, and I've borrowed one of my mother's matching necklaces. The jewels shimmer under the chandelier in my bedroom. I clutch a silk purse that Arturo gave me years ago.

Arturo, give me strength tonight.

Surprisingly, or perhaps not surprisingly, my mother's eyes flashed when I showed her the photo of Jack with a Nazi. "I don't blame you for wanting to go," she murmured. "But we put that relationship to rest a long time ago. Don't think that he has changed."

I paint my lips with scarlet lipstick, I have already painted my nails. My feet are encased in a pair of my mother's high heels. We have always been the same size, the same height, but so different in our outlooks. I always felt I was letting her down.

The irony is that people who don't know me think that I am like her. I know that there are those in Tuscany who see me as untouchable, elegant, unreachable. But the truth is, I have learned to play my cards close to my chest.

Mario is perched on a silk chair in my private sitting room, tentatively eating a bowl of broth and some bread. Every now and then he looks up to check I'm still here, and he has peppered me with questions ever since he woke. Are we staying here? Do I know where Signora Talia is? What will I do to find her? Do I think she's safe? Why are the Nazis in Venice? And then, quietly, there are his stories about his friends who he hasn't seen for months.

He bows his head and clams up when I ask him about them.

I only wish that, as an adult, I had answers, but the sad truth is that I have as many questions as he does, if not more.

I walk over to him, crouch down next to his chair. Touchingly, he reaches out and pats the elaborate hairstyle that my mother's elderly maid has spun out of my blond hair, threading it with jewels, while my mother looked on and told me that she hoped I made the most of the chance to mingle with men my own age.

I asked her if she would like me to bring a Nazi home for supper.

At that, she turned around and walked out of the room.

"When will you be back, signora?" Mario asks. He glances anxiously at the golden clock on the mantelpiece. His face has the ashen, harried look of someone much older. There is a paleness around his mouth, his smooth forehead is worried by a frown, and his eyes dart around constantly, watching for me, keeping me in his sights.

Poor boy. I am tempted to reach out and stroke his pale cheek, but I don't, not yet. I don't want to frighten him any further, and goodness knows, I do not want to replace Talia in his affections. I want to find his teacher, to reunite them, to establish what has happened to his parents.

I remove my wristwatch, stand up and place it on the coffee

table between the sofas in my living room. "There," I say. "My watch is one of the most precious things I own. My late husband gave it to me, but I'll leave it with you, so that you know I'm coming home."

He places his spoon back down. "My teacher would have come back to me if she could have."

The honesty in his voice tears at my heart. "I'm going to find her, Mario."

He looks at me, his lips curved downwards, his huge eyes narrowed. "And my parents, signora? Will you look for them too?"

The room feels overheated. I reach for a cigarette on the mantelpiece, frown at myself in the mirror above it. "Of course, I'll look for them." I eye him through the mirror. "I promise you; I will leave no stone unturned."

"Thank you, signora," he says gravely, and he picks up his spoon. "My mama is Fedora Di Maggio, and my father's name is Lino." His mouth sags again. "They... Every night I pray for them. I only want to see them again. That would make me happy."

I nod, trying and failing to rein in my emotions. "And you last saw your teacher right before the Germans came? She had you hiding in her house?"

Mario nods solemnly. He starts shivering. "But my parents never came for me. They never came."

"I know." I pick up a soft blanket from one of the sofas, move over to him, drape it across his shoulders, and now, silently, I take his hand and hold it. His nails are bitten down to the quick.

And we sit there, a middle-aged woman and a small boy, both of us lost, both of us wanting answers but not knowing where to find them.

Right now she is missing. I don't know where she is. I don't know where to start. But the beginning feels like a good place, and in the beginning of my adult life in Venice, there was Jack. Somehow, I need to establish whether he too is an enemy in a city where I feel like I have only one true friend.

I moor *Mimi* at the dock closest to the entrance of the Hotel Danieli, stepping carefully in my high heels in order to climb the marble steps into the hotel's stunning salon. If it were not replete with Nazis standing around like odious statues, one could be forgiven for thinking that there was no war at all.

The fourteenth-century Palazzo Dandolo, which has been part of the hotel since it opened in the 1820s and later welcomed Dickens, Wagner, Proust, and Charlie Chaplin, is lit up by the magnificent Murano glass chandeliers with no regard for blackouts, even though twilight is descending on the city. Clearly, the local Nazis are not worried about air raids and are trusting in the agreement that was wrought on both sides to protect Venice.

The pink marble panels and columns that stretch up to the vast decorated ceilings are polished to a sheen, and the gold and pale blue upholstered furniture is more resonant of the Napoleonic era than Hitler's intimidating and austere modern style. The chandeliers throw golden magic onto the walls that are made entirely of stained Murano glass circles, and a chamber orchestra are playing the overture to *Cosi fan Tutti*.

I announce myself to the doorman, who instantly lets me in when I state my title. I was prepared to tell him that I was Remo and Francesca Orlandi's daughter as well as the Contessa Messina, but it seems that my late husband holds enough cachet for him.

I slip over to the side of the magnificent foyer so that I can peruse the guests.

An elderly waiter appears with crystal goblets of champagne. "Dinner will be served at six o'clock, in the ballroom," he tells me. "The menu consists of Blanchailles au Citron, Poulet en casserole, and Asperge Hollandaise with Fraise a la Crème. The music program to accompany the meal will begin with Liszt's Hungarian Dances. As you see, standards are being upheld at the Danielli."

As the waiter moves on, I raise a brow. No Italian would be seen dead eating dinner at six o'clock.

A pair of middle-aged officers are already eyeing me as if I'm the whitebait instead of the Blanchailles, their smiles knowing behind their champagne and canapés.

The two Nazis approach me, predictably, and formally ask for my name. I toy with the idea of making up an alias and am running through ideas when my lips freeze.

Jack Sabo is standing across the crowded room, twenty-three years older than when I last saw him, among a group of men out of uniform. Newsmen, I imagine. The Nazis are more than willing to allow select foreign correspondents into their midst, as long as they tell one side of the story. Theirs. One story for the world, another reality for those living under their regime.

Our eyes catch, mine and Jack's. He blinks those curving green eyes, turns away quickly, looks at me again, and then, shaking his head, he whispers a comment in the ear of the Nazi nearest him, presses a hand to the man's shoulder, and strides across the room toward me.

"Lina."

He's next to me, but everything is too blurred for me to see him properly, and the room has turned fuzzy; the Nazis in uniform, the well-turned-out women, rendered indistinct.

"Lina," he murmurs, and it's that slow, soft voice he always reserved for me. Or I thought he did. Maybe I was mistaken. Maybe he also uses it to court Nazi favors. I shudder.

I take a sip of my champagne, but it is cold as a snake down my throat, and the nerves in my fingers tingle. I take him in.

Lemon-scented cologne, tanned cheeks, square jawline, slight dint beneath his bottom lip.

"This is no place for you." His voice is even deeper, richer, now, although it was always sonorous and low, and as his lips curve downward that indentation deepens. "But it's good to see you. Always."

Sea, sun, summer. Our hands encircled, that tingling running up my arm, we jump the tiny, sun-spun wavelets at the Lido, running out to sea, swimming together in the privacy afforded by the water, falling into the curve of each other's arms, the tingling all over now, him holding me gently, buoyant, and intimately out in the water as if I'm as light as air. Our eyes clashing, my body turning to his and my arms around him as naturally as water lapping against the soft arc of the sand, our lips always so close but not daring to touch, even out here, in the sea.

But now, I'm no longer that inexperienced girl standing opposite a devastatingly good-looking man in a grand hotel. I run a business, look after staff, keep my tenant farmers and their families safe and fed. I am a mother, albeit not a perfect one; I am the Contessa Messina, and the most important thing to me now is finding Talia.

I am not the pretty young Evelina Orlandi. She does not exist anymore, and, oh, how I had to battle to let her go. He cannot bring her back. She's gone. We're gone. Two decades ago.

"I thought you wrote the stories, rather than featuring in them."

That dint beneath his bottom lip deepens as it always did when he was agitated.

A bald, middle-aged Nazi marches over to us. He is short, with a broad chest and a gleam in his small eyes.

"Herr Sabo," the Nazi says to Jack. "You are speaking with the most beautiful woman in the room."

Odiously, the man picks up my hand and places his moist lips on my wrist.

I recoil. Any frisson that I was feeling at being close to Jack dissipates like bathwater down a drain.

"I am entranced by your magical city, but more so by this enchanting woman. Who is she?" he asks Jack, talking right over my head.

I reach out and place the champagne on a nearby table before I throw it all over both of them, but the Nazi doesn't let go of my other hand.

"This is Contessa Evelina Messina," Jack says, enunciating my title so slowly that I feel a brush scraping through my insides. I realize with a jolt he must know who I am—who I became. "Contessa, this is Herr Wilhelm Moritz, the commander of Venice."

I nod at the Nazi, ignoring the irony in Jack's tone. Here then is the man who was shaking Jack's hand on the newspaper's front page. I may have married a count, but they are both snakes.

I feel Jack's eyes burn into me and I push my shoulders back and stand tall.

"You are Venetian?" Wilhelm Moritz asks.

I open my mouth, unwilling to commit to being anything to this man, when another Nazi wearing the insignia of the Grand Admirals shouts for our attention across the room, and Wilhelm Moritz lets go of my hand. As he leaves us, I pick up a napkin from the table and wipe my hand over and over again.

Jack waits for me to walk with him into the grand ballroom.

"How are you, Lina?" he asks, his voice low.

"I was better, before I saw you on the cover of the newspaper shaking hands with a Nazi."

He stiffens beside me. "So, that's why you're here."

I bark out a dry laugh. "That, and the fact that Talia has

disappeared. Remember her? You once told her that you loved her like a sister, and that you loved me like—"

"I remember." He grinds out the words. "Has she been deported?"

The question is so perfunctory that I stop dead. "I thought you might know."

He glares straight ahead. The crowd thickens around us, men simper away in German, laugh revoltingly, women sprinkle laughter into the conversations, and we walk with them into the ballroom where I had my first dance at the age of sixteen.

The grand room is darkened, and one side of it is set up with rows of red velvet seats behind which there is a film projector. I can't help but remember the first time I met Jack, in another crowded ballroom, all those years ago.

Reluctantly, I sit down on the edge of a row, perching on my seat and glancing around. If I was a cat, I'd be twitching my tail.

Jack slides into the seat next to me, and next to him sits a man in the uniform of the SS. I stare straight ahead, forcing myself to stay seated when I want to run out of the room. Jack chats easily with the Nazi and I tug at the sleeve of my mother's dress, my hands smoothing the velvet over and over. I wasn't ready to see him. And I certainly wasn't ready for this. Nothing could have prepared me for the sight of a man I once loved working side by side with the Nazis. And yet, here we are.

Suddenly, a wave of nausea passes through me. I need to know where Talia is, and I need to find out tonight. If I don't, these odious men will place her on a train to Poland and she won't live.

Agitated, I cross and uncross my legs, open my purse, snap it closed again.

"You look well," Jack murmurs, turning away from the Nazi. "The fashion for military dresses suits you."

"At least I'm not wearing a swastika."

Jack opens his mouth, but Wilhelm Moritz, the commander

of Venice, heaven help us, comes to the front of the room, and snaps his feet together. Heil Hitler. Everyone in the room follows suit, including Jack. Except me.

Moritz talks for a while in rapid German, and the audience leans forward, folded hands, eyes on fire, listening to him. I've never been in the presence of a room of Nazis before, and the experience unnerves me.

The screen behind Wilhelm Moritz comes to life. Numbers roll down from ten to one, and after a spiel in German, we are treated to images of a joyous camp for Jewish "refugees."

I cover my mouth with my hand. Children are splashing around in swimming pools, girls dressing blond dolls, boys playing hide-and-seek on a grassy knoll. There is a table groaning with healthy food, dark German bread, oranges, and jugs of fresh milk. Women serve the children. They are being reformed, rehabilitated, taken care of. *Taken care of.* I understand enough German to feel my body turn cold, as if someone has just splashed a jug of icy water down my arms and into my soul. It's all lies.

I send a sidelong glance to the SS officer. My heartbeat pounds at the sight of the satisfied, gloating expression on his face. His hands rest on his knees, and he leans forward, tapping his foot in time with Wagner's *Die Meistersinger von Nürnberg.*

I move to stand up. I will be sick if I stay here.

But Jack places a firm hand on my knee.

It is electric. I take in a shaking breath.

He glances at me and shakes his head. "Don't," he mouths. "Wait."

I swallow roughly, my stomach swirling with the treacherous champagne I accepted from the Nazis, and I stay in my seat. *What am I doing here? What was I thinking? Why did I come?*

Jack was trouble from the moment I laid eyes on him. We were trouble, a shipwreck headed for the nearest jagged rock.

Why on earth I thought I could come here and make him see reason, I don't understand. I've wasted a precious evening, when I should have been looking for Talia, searching the city, asking questions... but of whom? And what should I ask?

The audience claps politely, the ladies' silk-gloved hands making a light patter in the gorgeous room when the film comes to a crackling end. The men stand up and begin thumping each other on the backs and exclaiming in cheerful German. I stand up and Jack places a hand on my back. I am more than happy to be steered out of this room.

"I'll walk you to a taxi." Jack is close behind me. "I'm sorry you are so upset."

"Upset?" I turn to him. "It was a mistake coming here."

"Wait." He stops at the end of the row, our bodies brushing. "You came here to see me?"

I feel my face burning. I clutch my purse tightly to my waist and pull my other arm away from him. "Clearly, there is nothing left to say. Except goodbye."

He mouths something, but then shrugs and walks me to the dock outside the magnificent entrance to the hotel. I only sense him stiffen a little when he lays eyes on *Mimi* where she is moored among the glittering boats the Nazis have stolen. Stolen from Jewish families like the Baruchs. The reflections of the lights from the hotel on the water swirl like a thousand fireflies in front of my eyes. I move toward *Mimi*, my hand plunging into my purse for my keys.

He's standing there in the dark while I grasp *Mimi*'s keys like a lifeline, and for a moment I'm tricked into thinking that the silhouette is the man I knew all those years ago. But you can't bring back the past.

"I don't know what to say, Lina."

I draw in a few slow breaths. "Then help me. Where are they keeping the Jewish families?" I ask him, my voice barely audible over the lapping of the water against the dock. A quintessentially Venetian sound. "Tell me, Jack, or I go to the commander first thing in the morning. Ask him myself. Tell me, what odious holding place are they using to keep my..." tears glitter in my eyes, "*our* old friend before throwing her in a cattle truck and deporting her to hell."

The dint beneath his lips deepens. His green eyes flash and he throws a hand up and wipes it over his immaculate brown hair, but he doesn't say anything.

"Tell me. Did you photograph them taking her away? Tell the story back in Germany?"

"Lina, how could you *think* I would know?"

"Where are they holding her?" My voice cuts through the air and he turns away.

A cold breeze springs up from the dark water that runs beneath us.

"Tell me," I say, my breaths catching and hitching.

Another couple approaches the dock. My keys are cold in my hands.

I focus on Jack. "You are not walking away. Tell me the truth. If that is not too difficult this time," I whisper. "No excuses."

"I never gave you an excuse." He turns back to face me.

"True. You just left. How many ways can you let people down, Jack?"

I wait. The couple, German, laughing, are closer toward us.

Jack glances back at them.

"Scared of betraying them?" I whisper. "Jack. Where have they all been sent? You must know," I hiss.

The German couple come to a halt in front of us. "The Jews? They are in the women's prison at Giudecca," the Nazi says. "It's no secret. We are taking regular transports to Poland as scheduled. Everything is going to plan."

His companion simpers up at him and he pats her on the bottom.

I want to be ill. I clutch at the guard rope, my feet sliding on the ramp. In an instant, Jack is there next to me, and even though I try to push him away, he stays with me until I am steady.

"Goodbye, Jack."

"Keep away, Lina." He whispers this softly, but the warning is evident.

"Oh, don't you worry. I will."

I wrench myself away and climb into *Mimi*, my emotions all over the place.

Once I'm clear of the dock, I turn around briefly. Jack is standing in front of the hotel, a silhouette, perfectly still. A man I don't know anymore. A man whom I must not trust. A man I once thought I knew better than myself.

CHAPTER 8

I do not sleep, or if I do, it is fitful and restless. After checking that Mario is sleeping soundly in the room next to mine, I lie on my back most of the night, the curtains thrown open so the reflection of the Grand Canal in the moonlight shimmers on the ceiling, dances between the cornices, floats around the roses and ivy that are intertwined around the chandelier. The gold and diamond watch that Arturo gave me for my thirtieth birthday glints in the moonlight on my bedside table. The silk nightdress he bought me is tangled around my legs and pools over my body.

Eventually, I turn onto my side, wrapping my arms around my body in the way I did after Arturo died, in the way I did after my relationship ended with Jack.

As much as I loved Arturo and miss him, there was something that I cannot put my finger on about that summer spent with Jack. The three of us—he, Talia, and I—were as tight as a tapestry, and there was a magic about being with them, as if something wonderful was always around the next corner, and we were chasing it, together. I thought, naively, that I would spend the rest of my life with Jack. I had a hazy plan, either he would stay in Venice, or I would go to New York. I imagined me meeting his family in Cincinnati. Like Jack, his father was a newspaper man who had studied at Harvard. He'd come from a wealthy Italian family here in Venice, migrated to America with his brothers, and they'd remained a tight-knit, close unit. Jack had grown up in a sprawling house with two sisters, and aunts and uncles visiting constantly. He'd told me stories of how his parents would sit around the kitchen table and debate the news of the day. How his mom encouraged him to make something of himself, how she tutored him in history, English, math, and science, supporting him, alongside his adored father, to go to Harvard and study journalism like his dad.

He was always so informed, so well read, so street smart. But, has he, like my parents did, decided to take the easy road through the war? The path of least resistance, curling up in a basket with the snakes?

I prop myself up on my fist. A boat chugs past my window. A shout in angry German pierces the night air. My mouth twists into a grimace, and I stand up, pace around my bedroom, lean heavily against the windowsill and gaze out at the shadowy water, watching the boat make its way down the canal, waiting, sleepless, for morning to arrive; dreading it, for I know what I must do. Dreading what I'm going to find at the Giudecca prison where they are holding our Jewish population, where they are holding my very best friend.

The sun is sparkling, the Grand Canal is luminous. At first light, I walk through the cobbled lanes to the Basilica San Marco. If the exterior of the church of Santa Maria della Salute is my friend in the distance, the interior of the Basilica San Marco is my spiritual home. The last time I was in the beautiful old church that graces the Piazza San Marco, a chamber orchestra was playing Vivaldi, and the lights were on, highlighting the golden mosaics in the cathedral's multitude of Byzantium domes. I had simply gone there for some peace and quiet during the war, and felt like I had entered into something magical. The music and the way the domes were lit up with all the old mosaics telling timeless stories gave me hope, and a connection to joy that I hadn't felt in a long while.

But now, the interior is dim after the brilliant sunshine outside, and I kneel down and pray that I will find Talia alive and safe. That, somehow, I can do something to help.

Back out in the square, children are feeding pigeons, throwing breadcrumbs and delighting in the way the birds flock around them, but their mothers stand about, wary, eyeing the Nazis who hover like statues on the corners. The soldiers hide under the arches of the grand buildings that used to house the offices of the government workers during the years of the doges, and now are probably taken up by Nazi officials.

I put my head down and walk back across the square. What will I find when I arrive at Giudecca prison? Will Talia be there? I have heard that there is a camp at Fossoli, north of Modena, which was an Allied prisoner of war camp during the early years of the war until the Nazis came to Italy this year and turned it into a holding camp where they are interning our Jewish citizens before they transfer them to Germany or Poland, so she may have already been moved away from Giudecca. There are stories out of France that tell of heads being shaved, inmates starving in the holding prisons before they are transported to the camps. I try to focus on the sound of my footsteps, but my stomach is fluttering, and there is an emptiness inside me that will not budge.

It was in September that Professor Giuseppe Jona, the leader of the Jewish population of Venice, committed suicide rather than give the Nazis a list of Jewish citizens of Venice, and in this brave act, he saved many of our community. Most of the remaining Jewish population have escaped by now, but what of those who didn't want to leave their home or weren't able to?

Back at home, I slip down to the landing dock out front of the palazzo, having avoided my parents and ensured Mario was comfortable, fed and playing with some of my children's old toys. I steer *Mimi* along the small canals and into the San Marco basin, leaving the dramatic beauty of San Marco Piazza behind me as I move toward the Giudecca canal.

I moor her in a quiet spot near the women's prison, and I sit there for a moment, unnaturally still, my hands clamped tightly together. But there is no relief for my nervousness.

I walk, gathering my coat around me, following the line of the forbidding prison, windows barred and menacing, until I reach the solid entrance door.

Two Nazis stand at attention outside.

"*Buongiorno,*" I say, holding my head up, knowing that my blond hair is glistening in the sun. If they really want to adulate me for the way I look, then let them. I am more than happy to exploit that if it means I can help my friend.

One of the young Nazis carries out their odious salute to Hitler. Tells me in rough German that I need to move on.

And then it happens. An old vaporetto trawls up the canal toward the prison. Several Nazis stand to attention at the front of the boat. And, as if in slow motion, the vaporetto pulls up right opposite the front entrance to the prison, and the Nazi guards yell at me to get out of the way.

I step aside, and to my horror, the formidable prison doors open, and two more guards emerge. They stand aside, and then a bedraggled, tragic line of women appear, blinking in the sunlight, several of them holding the hands of children, some with babies on their hips. Elderly women are supported by younger women, and others hold the arms of young mothers-to-be, to help them maintain their balance as they appear to be too weak to move properly.

Their silhouettes are already gaunt beneath their striped prison garments. Paper-thin arms poke out from too-thin sleeves, and some of them have had their heads shaved, their eyes are dull, and their lips are ringed with the whiteness of fatigue.

If Mario's troubled, conflicted expression worried me, this sickens me to the core. I stagger backwards, my mouth falling open in disbelief at the way they are all herded onto the waiting vaporetto. Desperately, I eye the figures, searching for Talia, hoping at the same time to see her, and dreading it, only to spot someone else I recognize. My heart goes to my mouth and I move forward quickly.

The Nazis are so focused that they do not notice me moving toward one of the women, gently taking her arm, holding her close for a moment, the stink of her sweat, the skeletal-like feel of her frame against mine. I want to spit in these men's faces.

"Esther," I say. She is a friend of Talia's. She is recognizable, but notably diminished in weight and her bony shoulders are bowed, her dark eyes look hollow and her cheeks are streaked with dirt. Tears prick the backs of my eyelids, and my chest aches.

"They do not have Talia," Esther whispers. "She is not here."

I slump against her a moment. I want to take Esther away with me, but it is impossible; we are surrounded. In a flash of inspiration, I pull a piece of paper and a pen from my handbag. "Write down the name of every station that you pass on your journey. When you get to your final destination, throw the paper out the window of the train, and put my name and address on it. I will help you as soon as it comes back to me, Esther. I will do everything I can."

A Nazi shouts and we pull apart. Esther bows her head and furtively takes the paper, as she moves back, her head bowed. I stand there, my arms wrapped around my body, and I watch the tragic parade of innocent women and children help each other as they go to meet their fates.

CHAPTER 9

After my visit to the Giudecca prison, I am being meticulous with Mario, keeping him away from the windows, drawing the curtains and not letting him outside. My parents and I are living with an uneasy truce. I know they will not report him, but I know that I have a time limit for keeping the child in their home.

I have made lists of old friends of Talia's family. The problem is these friends of hers are Jewish. In order to try to obtain some authoritative information, I listen assiduously to the BBC radio service from England. This is, of course, illegal, but it's something I have done since the war began.

One report has stated that elderly Jews and those who cannot work are being shot immediately on arrival in the labor camps in the Soviet Union and Poland, that they are being forced to dig their own graves before being executed. There is a camp out of Warsaw that we are starting to understand is the worst camp. At night, I toss and turn, worrying that Talia was already deported to this terrifying camp by the time I arrived at Giudecca.

While I am anxious about Talia, I worry about what Raf is

witnessing, how he is coping. He is far more sensitive than Nico. I have not had a letter from Raf in weeks. I worry too about Cara managing in Tuscany on her own. I speak with her daily, and the lovely girl insists that she is fine. That she, my cook Bettina, and Alphonso can run the estate between them. I concede that they probably can. It is I who am not getting anywhere. And not getting anywhere does not sit well with me.

I am sitting reading to Mario in Nico's old bedroom where I have settled him now, when my father appears at the door.

"Can I speak with you?"

I nod, and tuck little Mario up, blow out the candle by his bed, and wish him a peaceful night's rest. He seems to have grown a little calmer now.

I follow my father.

"You have news?" I ask him anxiously.

"Of sorts. I have news of Nico."

Once in his sitting room, I slump down on a chair. My feelings about my family are in turmoil. "Oh, Nico. Please," I ring my hands. "Tell me he is safe."

A line appears between my father's eyes. "He is doing business with the Nazis. Nico is in Milano, running a steel factory that—"

"Is producing ammunition for Hitler." I grimace. My eldest son.

"Nico is a pragmatist. But in this case..." My father lets out a heavy sigh. His voice cracks and he speaks slowly, as if taking great care to choose each word, knowing, perhaps, that what he says now could make or break our relationship, cause it to crack inexorably, to fragment to such an extent that it might never repair. "You know that I supported a stronger Germany after the Great War."

I stare at him.

"But our Jewish friends have been rounded up, people we have known for forty years taken away and separated from their families, grandchildren, daughters..." He shakes his head. "At night, all I do is pray for them. Men I used to meet in Café Florian for breakfast, men I worked with for decades, their wives, lovely women. All gone. All gone, and Hitler has betrayed those of us who believed in him. And there is nothing to be done. I had no idea that humans were even capable of what we are seeing happening at this time. And we can't stop it. I don't know what to say about Nico." His shoulders slump heavily and his face is blank. "I'm sorry, darling."

I stand up, walk over to him, and clasp his hand. "In this case," I say, "my son's behavior is morally reprehensible, Papa."

My father tightens his grip on my hand. He closes his eyes as if he's trying to process what this means. My son, working with the enemy.

And Jack, mingling with the Nazis right under our noses.

There are meant to be two sides in war. But how are you supposed to deal with the fact that people you loved, or once loved and trusted, might not have ever been who you thought they were?

Out in the back garden, a mist hangs over the leafless trees. The air seems to whisper around me as if it is mourning too, and I feel the same sad sensation that I sensed in Talia's parents' garden in her *sestiere*. A dog barks in the distance. Venice feels immeasurably cold.

I beat back the shame I feel about Nico. The little boy I carried, raised to the best of my ability, clearly could not turn into a decent human being.

In all my thinking over the past few days, in all my hopeless-ness after witnessing that awful sight of women and children being transported, trying to track them on the map, and hoping, hoping, that the measly piece of paper that I gave Esther might in some miraculously different world, come back to me, I have discovered only one good thing. One beacon of hope shining brightly.

Among acquaintances and friends I heard whispers of the nuns and priests of Venice hiding those Jews who did not make it out before the new decree. I hold on to this like a lifebuoy, hoping Talia may still be here.

I am going to act upon this hope. I am going to visit every church in Venice, every single one.

CHAPTER 10

The following evening, Papa and I are in his sitting room. At dinner, my mother was tight-lipped about my son, but something else was bothering them. I could sense it, feel it. But they said nothing. Now, Papa wants to talk to me, and we have been making awkward conversation, both of us skirting around the topic of Nico. More than ever, I feel that I have done something wrong as a mother when it comes to my son.

And then, Papa hits me with something worse.

"The Nazis are after the child," he says without any preamble. "They will strike, but they are waiting for the opportunity to do so. And there is a complication." Papa leans forward in his chair and rests the glass of whiskey between his knees.

I am indignant. My eyes flash fire. "Well, they take him over my dead body. What possible threat could he be to the Third Reich? And how do they know where Mario is?"

"They know everything. Mario's bloodlines risk..." Papa has the grace to redden. The grace to meet my eyes, and finally, I see the expression in them that I've longed for ever since I arrived home. It is something that I know is buried deep within him, that he holds back in the name of appeasing my mother, of being the aristocrat he is supposed to be. But now, I sag with relief. Because in his eyes I can sense empathy. Finally. *Finally.* "They say the child is poisoning the pure population. Their Aryan bloodline. That is what they are puffing themselves up about." Papa sits back in his seat and crosses his legs. "I have also asked around and learned some more about the child."

I frown at him. The spy during the Great War, who passed naval intelligence to the British via secret messages. Sometimes I underestimate my father. He can be hard to read, hard to understand, but I do know that when push comes to shove, I can rely on him.

"Yes?" I ask.

"His parents were... or are left-wing activists."

"So that must be why they left Mario with Talia. It would have been too dangerous to have a child with them."

"According to the intelligence I have, it seems likely that Mario's mother and father have been interred in the Soviet Union in one of the camps." He takes in a deep breath. "The Germans are reserving the worst atrocities for *outside* their country, Evie."

I worried that they must have been transported. This goes along with what I have heard illegally on the BBC about the camp in Poland. "But why have the Nazis not taken Mario from the palazzo if they want him so badly? If that really is their focus, then why do they delay?" Fear stirs in my gut.

I stand up. I need air. I take a turn around the room and lean on the back of Papa's chair.

He reaches up and takes my hand. " At the moment, Wilhelm Moritz thinks they are being reasonable by making a concession. He is waiting gracefully for us to hand the child over when we see good sense. He is being civilized, he says. Because we are aristocracy."

Ah, yes, Wilhelm Moritz. The man whom Jack introduced

me to at the Danieli. The commander of Venice. I tighten my grip on my father's hand. I need one member of my family to be on my side in this.

"So, they will start playing a game of cat and mouse with you until you break."

"A game?"

Papa nods. "They are already following you. Soon, they will make it *clear* they are doing so. You will become terrified, and give up the child as a bargaining tool for them to leave you alone."

My stomach clenches.

"You won't be able to get the child out of the palazzo, even if you want to. They are everywhere. I'm afraid, as I said, it's a game of cat and mouse and you are the mouse."

I am silent.

"*We* are the mice," my father says quietly.

I sit next to him on the sofa and he takes me in his arms.

Later, we are still ensconced in Papa's sitting room. My mother drifted in a while ago, announcing she was going to bed. My father and I are going around in circles, he wanting to protect me, while I am certain that I have to find Talia, both of us agreeing that we must shield Mario at all costs. I tell him of what I witnessed at Giudecca. How I cannot live with myself unless I do everything I can.

Finally, my father frowns. "I think they are waiting for an opportune time. For a slip-up, possibly to see if you lead them to Talia, because I think she is whom they are really after."

I stop pacing relentlessly around the room. "You think she may still be at large?" I circle back to the stories of the nuns and the priests in the churches. And then, has she left the city? If she has escaped? But would she go far unless she knew Mario was safely back with his parents? That is what I doubt.

"I'm beginning to think she could be," Papa says.

"Because for the moment, they are allowing the child to remain in my house." He raises his eyes to meet mine where I am standing. "Remember, they are in control, not you. I know how much you hate that."

I lift my chin.

"But you can't run things, Evie. You have no free agency in this regime. And you may well not be able to fix this situation."

"I have to."

Papa leans forward on the sofa, cradles his whiskey. "They know exactly what you are doing."

I heave out a sigh and stare at the ceiling.

"Darling, they are trusting in the fact that you will lead them to Talia. If they capture you, they reduce their chance of finding Talia, you see."

"Let's go back to what you told me when I first came to Venice. This is placing Mother and you in danger. Papa, I can move out…"

Gently, he takes my shoulders and looks into my eyes. "I know what I am doing. And I'm with you. All I want is for you to be safe. Leave the boy here. There is nothing to be gained by moving him. And one more thing."

I nod and hold his blue-eyed gaze. Mirror to mirror, he always understood me well.

"I don't want your heart to be broken for the third time. You have more than enough to worry about with Talia, Mario, and Nico. Don't get involved in anything else. Promise me."

Jack.

There is a silence.

I sit down and stare blankly at the untouched glass of white wine on the coffee table in front of me. I place my head in my hands.

This is the torture the Nazis have placed upon us all. Their power lies in us not knowing whether or not our loved ones are safe. Not being sure who we can trust. Their control comes in watching our every move. In us knowing they are doing so. In us knowing we can do nothing about it. In the silence they weave around us like spiders.

And Jack is working with them. Spreading lies.

"I am not about to have an affair with Jack." I grind out the words. "It was over years ago. And we are no longer on the same side."

Papa moves across to the drinks cabinet and pours himself another whiskey.

"Tomorrow, I go to the churches to pray," I say. "I will pray in every church, every nunnery in this city until I find her."

Or not.

Neither of us say the words, but they hover in the air, and crackle in the fire that flickers in the grate.

CHAPTER 11

It is, after all, the seventh anniversary of my late husband's death. So, I beg his forgiveness for what I am doing, but each morning, I leave the house in black. I go to the churches in Venice and pray for my Arturo's soul, kneeling in the front pews, speaking afterward with the clergy in order to ascertain whether or not their church might be privy to helping a Jewish woman. Their answers to my questions about how the Germans are treating the Jews are varying. Many of them appear too scared to comment. Like Pope Pius XII, they prefer to remain silent about the latest Nazi decrees. In some churches, I strike outright anti-Semitism.

It is in the church of San Giacomo di Rialto that a most extraordinary thing happens while I am praying, and in my agitated state about Talia's safety, I wonder whether I am hallucinating.

Inside the old church, the air is fragrant with the incense of a recent service, and there is that misty quality reaching up to the lofty ceiling, which only incredibly old churches in late fall or winter can bring.

I am already concerned because this is day five of my prayer sessions, and I have learned nothing helpful so far. Outside the dimly lit church, the sun is shining over Venice, and it is so like the beautiful day in Tuscany when my husband died in my arms after he had suffered a heart attack in the garden. I miss him terribly today.

I am murmuring the same prayers that I have every day this week, thanks for Arturo's life, blessings, and safety for Talia, praying to God to protect her, wherever she is. Knowing that he will not mind if she is Jewish.

I pray silently for Nico too.

It is right then that something brushes my shoulder. The feeling is soft, too soft for a hand, but heavier than a feather, and I frown.

I ignore whatever it is for a moment, assuming that a light breeze is floating in through an open window. But there it is again, and I turn to have a look.

Incredibly, a piece of paper is brushing against my sweater. I stare incredulously, because the small piece of paper is hanging from a string that is suspended from the ceiling. I look up. The string appears to be protruding down from one of the lights. But the ceiling is so lofty that I have to squint to be able to see what is going on. After a few moments of abject staring, I realize that the string has been suspended not from the light, but from an elegant grille around it.

And then, my heart almost stops.

The paper has writing on it, and the writing is Talia's, or I am utterly losing my mind. In the dim light, I reach out to grasp it. It is real. I hold it between the thumb and forefinger of my right hand. As subtly as possible, I detach the odd little page from the string, and put it in the pocket of my woolen skirt.

I glance around quickly, but there is no indication that anyone has witnessed this strange event. The church remains silent. My heart feels like it has jumped up into my mouth, and the string on which the paper was hanging ascends back up to the ceiling, from whence it came.

I am astounded. It takes all my willpower not to stare at the string as it floats upwards to the rafters, hoping to see Talia's face through the roof looking down on me. The grille is patterned with F holes like those on a violin, and as if by magic, the string disappears into the cavity of the ceiling.

I place my right hand into the pocket of my skirt, and my fingers curl around the paper and stay there.

On the way out of the church to the old piazza, I risk a glance at the roof, in disbelief.

I walk back out of the square toward the Rialto Bridge and home, not turning to look back at the church of San Giacamo di Rialto. I keep my eyes trained on the path ahead.

It is not until I am in the privacy of my bedroom that I close the curtains, turn on the light, and sit down on the bed. My hands are shaking as I open up the piece of paper. It is definitely written in Talia's handwriting. My hand covers my mouth as I read the message. She refers to me as Nina, and this name she called me is only something she and I shared.

Nina,

Please don't worry. I am safe.

T.

I sit with this note from my best friend, relief washing over me. But how on earth can Talia be safe in a city overrun by Nazis? My father warns they will be following me in order to find Talia. Have I played right into the Nazis' hands? I stand up, go to my dressing table, light a candle, and burn the note.

. . .

Later that night, I dress in a pair of flared black trousers and a black polo-neck jumper. A mask is in my hand. As I step out of the palazzo to the Grand Canal, I feel everything. This is forbidden. It is impossibly dangerous. If I am caught, I will be incarcerated and shot.

I crouch down and make my way through the back alleyways of Venice, following my nose, until I arrive in the *sestiere* of San Polo. My feet beat a rhythm on the wet cobblestones, and I am propelled only by one thought. Get to Talia. That must be my focus. The words of her telegram are like a fire in my mind. I cannot give up on her, no matter what she said in this note. I need to see her. Nothing else but that.

In another ten minutes, I am safely in the silent square that houses the church of San Giacamo di Rialto. I slip into the cover provided between two buildings, lurking in the shadows like a thief. The old portico runs across the front of the church as it has since the eleventh century, and the narrow windows that are set into the roof cavity are black as ink.

But then my eyes widen in disbelief, in incredulity, as two nuns in habits, one carrying a ladder, carefully close the door to the church, creep around the side and come to a stop beneath the portico. They put up the ladder, one checks that it is sound, and the other, whom I notice is carrying a basket, hoists up her habit and begins climbing the rungs to the roof of the church. My heart thumps with every step she takes, and my eyes are glued rigidly to her back.

This must be how they are feeding Talia, and whoever else is up there. It will be freezing up in the roof cavity. The nights are getting colder, and she will be living in Venice's damp without any protection. I have to get her out.

The second nun stands guard over the square as the first nun creeps along the top of the portico, the window to the roof of the church opens, and she disappears, basket and all.

I take in a ragged breath, remove my mask and shake my

hair loose so that the nun on the ground will know I am female, and I walk toward the church, right through the middle of the square.

"Hello," I whisper, when the nun's hand goes to her heart at the sound of my footsteps, alarm distorting her features. She staggers backwards but keeps a firm grip on the ladder, and she crosses herself with her free hand. "It is all right," I say to her, still keeping my voice low. "I am the Contessa Messina, and I am a friend of Talia Baruch."

The nun eyes me warily.

"Talia is, in fact, my oldest friend, and I have searched all of Venice to find her. Today, I learned that she was here. Please. Let me help you."

The nun is still silent. Her gaze swivels up to the roof. I understand. I have the blond hair and the appearance that the Nazis want to bottle. I hardly look like a friend. What's more, the Germans are sending infiltrators in to catch people unawares. She is right not to trust me.

"Talia got a note to me while I was praying in the church. She lowered it down via a piece of string."

The nun finally takes the note, reads it, and nods her head. "It is how we told her to communicate with us, but only when the church is empty. My name is Sister Beatrice," she says, inclining her head in a sweet smile. She looks to be in her sixties, and she has button eyes and a kind face.

"Thank you, Sister Beatrice," I whisper. "May I?" I indicate up at the roof.

The nun looks in the same direction, worriedly. "Sì, but be careful, Contessa, the portico roof needs replacing."

With each step on the ladder, my stomach feels like it's falling to the ground. Will I make it to Talia at last?

CHAPTER 12

The roof cavity looks empty when I enter it. The stink of pigeon droppings infiltrates the air, and I wrap my coat closer around me. It is glacial up here. No light, windows that are cracked and dirty, bare floorboards. It is an attic space that is only fit for storage. And then my heart contracts. In a corner of the attic, farthest away from the cold air that sifts through the cracks and crannies, there is a small bed made up on the floor. Rough blankets are set neatly on what looks to me like a straw mattress. A wooden crate is turned upside down next to it, and on this, there is a jug of water, a covered plate.

The meal that the nun was bringing up. My eyes pool over as I stare helplessly at the way my friend has been living. How many other refugees from the Third Reich are living in the roof cavities of churches in Italy? I shudder to think.

"Talia?" I whisper into the emptiness. They would have heard my footsteps ascending the ladder, been terrified by the sound of me clambering along the portico's tiled roof. I take in a shaking breath, close my eyes. "Darling, it is me. Nina."

When Talia steps out from behind one of the heavy stone pillars that are dotted about the roof cavity, I let out a sob and almost fall toward her, folding her in my arms, my hand running through her hair. As I hold her, all the memories come flooding back, that little girl on the swing, the way she got me through when Arturo died.

But then she pulls back. Even in the dim, dust-filled air, I can tell that her usually sparkling eyes are huge and hollow in her pale cheeks, and her curls are plastered to the side of her face. Her hair looks damp. Cold, so cold. She reaches up to pull her hair away from her face with hands that are covered in fingerless gloves. Her whole body shakes and when I take her hands between mine, they are freezing and damp at the same time.

"Thank goodness you are safe. I'm here now. Come home with me. To Tuscany."

She stares at me for a moment, then glances away, shaking her head.

"Talia," I whisper. I press my hand into her bird-like arm. "I am here. I am here." It is all I can manage to utter. There are not the words.

But then, those huge, too big eyes rake over my face, the golden tinges in her irises flashing with that old fire that always drew me into its warmth. "I won't leave Venice. I can't. I only wanted to let you know I was safe today." She shakes her head and I glance at the top of the ladder. In spite of the cold up here, my body heats up underneath my coat, and I feel a flush creeping up through my face.

"No," I say, simply. "Come with me. *Mimi* and I will take you to the Villa Rosa." She is delirious, not thinking straight.

But her eyes dart toward the nun who has just broken cover too, and back to me again. "I can't leave Venice, Nina."

I glance around at the nun, who is moving slowly across the ghostly, dim space. She bends over the covered basket by the makeshift bed, pulls out the bread and broth that she has brought for Talia. "Please," she says. "You must eat, signora."

"Yes, yes," I urge, running my hands through my hair. "Please, eat your food." And then we will go.

I wrap my arms around my body, staring at the cold, dark space where Talia seems to want to stay. Images of the women being forced out of the Giudecca prison flood my mind. Cattle trucks. Camps. I shudder.

The nun holds out the mug of broth determinedly, her gaze focused on Talia.

Talia takes one last look at me, and then moves across the space, settles on the mattress, and eats the bread, drinks the broth, her head down.

A freezing shaft of air filters into the space and seems to seep into my bones.

The nun regards the watch that is pinned to the chest of her habit. "We have only a few minutes before they will come through the square. Their inspections run like clockwork. Their efficiency is saving her and allowing me to time things precisely," she whispers to me. "Giving us the chance to come to her each night."

I nod, taking in the kindly young nun's face, the doubtful expression in her eyes, the way she keeps glancing anxiously at the ladder.

Talia places the empty bowl back in the basket, covers it up again, and comes across the room to me. "Nina, I can't come with you. I'm not leaving Venice. I made a promise, and I won't break it."

I rub my hands together. There is not time for us to argue here. "No," I say. "You must come with me. You won't survive up here." My words come out harsher than I mean them to, and Talia takes a step back.

"I can't leave Venice," she repeats, her voice thin yet determined. "There is someone I will not leave."

I almost slump with relief. "Mario," I say. "Yes, yes, I have him safely."

"What? That cannot be. He should be..." She shakes her head. "With the Di Maggios."

"He is at home. Sleeping in Nico's old bed." My voice catches, but Talia looks away and starts rubbing her hands together, over and over.

"No," she murmurs. "No."

The nun picks up the basket and moves toward the window, her hands grasping the ladder firmly. "Please," she says. "I am going. I will not risk this any further."

Talia digs her hands into the pockets of her skirt, turns to me, her eyes flashing now. "What do you mean you have him? Why? Please. Where are his parents? Have they been taken? Do you know whether they are safe? This is a disaster. He loves them. Please!"

"He was hiding in the laundry chute." I wipe a stray tear from my eyes.

Talia pulls her hands out again, folding them through each other. "Please no," she whispers. "Not Fedora and Lino." Her eyes graze my face. "You don't understand. The Nazis will murder Mario. His parents are some of the most-wanted Jews in the city. I can't leave all of this and run away to Tuscany. Don't worry about me. I'm safe here. The only thing I can suggest is that you send Mario to me."

I reach out, freeing one hand from the incessant rubbing, warming it between my own hands. But she turns away from me.

There is something I cannot fathom here. Something I can't break through. "But I tell you, I'm not running away with you."

She pulls her hand away from mine. I hear the nun's voices, whispering softly below the ladder.

"Signora!"

The sound of the nun's agitated whisper filters up into the roof.

Suddenly, I reach out again and pull at Talia's hand. "Come with me. I will sort it all out for you."

"You can't fix this," she whispers, and her voice sears into my back as I haul her toward the ladder. "Just go."

I try to understand the expressions that pass across her face.

I can feel the tension emanating from the nuns down in the square.

"Either you stay here, and I stay with you, or we both go down," I say, eyeing her.

Talia glares at me a moment and shakes her head. "You don't understand," she barks out the words. "You could never."

I tip my head back. "No, but I know that I can take care of you. And Mario," I whisper.

She sends me a frightened glance, and I pull her to me, holding her close.

"Go, now," I whisper into her hair. "Just go down the ladder, and I will look after you both. Please."

She glances back at the dark makeshift mattress in the corner. "But if they have taken Mario's parents, then I should stay here."

I shake my head. Gently, I take her arm and lead her to the ladder. Goodness knows if I can get Talia and Mario to safety, but if there is one thing I've learned from this war, from all the loss, and the confusion and the complications, it is that I can rely on myself.

Once Talia is safely on the ladder, I step out into the night. The cold, dark air seems to loom around me, almost swallowing me. I only hope the faith that I have in myself is enough to get us through.

I grab Talia's hand as soon as I am on the ground next to her. She thanks the older Sister Beatrice and the other nun. Urgently, I lead Talia around the edge of the piazza, knowing instinctively exactly what route we will take back to the palazzo, hoping she will make it, as her whole body is shaking. She needs rest, sleep, food. I start moving instinctively. All I feel is overwhelming relief that she is safe. That I have her, despite her protestations. All I need to do now, is get her to the palazzo, inveigle her and Mario into *Mimi* and then take them to my car, and then the Villa Rosa.

When the gunshot rings out, cracking into the otherwise silent air, we are creeping around underneath the porticos of another building opposite the church.

I freeze, tightening my grip on Talia's hand. But at the same time, I whirl around to face the church, when Sister Beatrice falls to the ground.

I scream silently into my free hand.

"No," Talia whispers next to me. "No, that dear, kind nun. Oh, look what's happened now, Nina. You should have left me there!"

I am safe here. Don't take me out. Talia's words already bounce in my ears. I hold back a sob, and my stomach roils with anger, with guilt at what I've caused. Am I doing the wrong thing? Oh, how complicated is this war!

Wildly, needing to do something, anything, I press my balaclava into Talia's hands.

"Put it on," I whisper. "Wait here and give me two minutes."

My eyes are trained on the scene outside the church.

And then, it happens. There is a second gunshot. My skin feels like it is peeling off, but I lurch around to face Talia, and she is standing there, holding a little silver gun. She is quite still, staring at a point opposite us. No balaclava, as easy to identify as day. Some of that old determination is back in those dark eyes of hers.

I strain to see what she is staring at. And then, quickly, so quickly that I can hardly tell one second from the next, a man falls down on the far edge of the square. I gasp with horror. His own gun spins across the cobblestones, the metal ringing through the square sounding like the aftereffects of the gunshot. A pool of blood spills from his body, and within seconds, his chest is soaked. His legs shake a few times, and then he is motionless. In the darkness, I can see that his uniform is black.

Gestapo.

I rake over the square with my eyes, turn back to Talia. She's pulled on the balaclava, but is still standing there, staring at the Nazi she's just murdered.

In the distance, the younger nun who was up in the roof has Beatrice standing up and leaning on her shoulder. Thank goodness she is alive. They are moving back toward the church, disappearing inside the door.

Talia tucks the gun back in her pocket, only to pull it out again as a second man steps out from the shadows on the opposite side of the square behind the Nazi. My breathing hitches.

Talia points her gun at him.

"Darn you," she murmurs.

But as the second man walks out into the square and bends over the Nazi, Talia lowers her gun. She turns to me, her dark eyes blazing, golden hints of honeycomb glinting in the night.

"Is there something you haven't told me, Nina?"

But I only stare at her momentarily, before my eyes swivel back to the man squatting over the Nazi. And she puts her gun away and grabs my hand. I take a step forward, but Talia grabs my arm and pulls me back.

"Don't. Don't go near the scene. But I will be darned if I know why Jack Sabo is following you. I heard he was back, but you should know, he's on the other side."

I turn to her, then back to the figure that is now dragging the Nazi's body across the square, holding him by the underarms, while the man's head lolls to one side.

The square is closing in on me. My heartbeat is racing, and

my breath stalls as I stare at the figure on the other side of the square. Just as he reaches the cover of the opposing veranda, the man dragging the body stops, and for one moment, I'm sure he's staring at me.

I lurch out from under the cover of the veranda, only to feel Talia reeling me back in. But my eyes widen and lock with Jack's gaze. We are not in a crowded room, and I'm not wearing a ball gown, but in this dark, empty square, I'd still know him anywhere.

Talia's right. The man dragging the body of the Nazi away is Jack. But whose side is he on?

Minutes later, my fingers fumble with the key to the back gate of the palazzo. Behind me, Talia hides in the shadows across the laneway, seeming to be far more in control than me. Finally, the brass key clicks in the lock, and I push the door open. We creep past the gardener's cottage and into the misty, silent garden out back of my parents' home. The trees are still and eerie, the familiar shrubs and my old swing look strange. If the garden out the back of Talia's home felt like it was mourning the loss of its owners, my parents' garden feels loaded. It feels as if anyone, at any moment, could step outside with a gun.

My father told me that the Nazis were following me. Did they choose Jack for that role? I can't shake the image of him shaking hands with Wilhelm Moritz, of the odious way the commander of Venice spoke of me as if I were bait hanging on a fishhook. I can't shake the image of Jack sitting and smiling with them. But now, Talia's murdered a member of the Gestapo, and Jack's witnessed it. If he takes the body and reports her... the Nazis say they will kill ten Italians for every Nazi who dies.

As I lead Talia through my house, it is as if we are strangers in my own childhood home, and I dread one of my own parents appearing and telling us to leave.

Finally, we come to Nico's bedroom, where I've let Mario sleep. If my son does not want to talk to me, then I'll at least put his room to good use, help someone else in need. Talia walks in, and the moment her eyes land on Mario's little sleeping figure, she lets out a sob, and moves toward the sleeping boy.

She bends over him, resting her head on the blankets, her shoulders shaking, until she finally turns back to me, her pretty dark eyes smiling. "Thank you," she whispers. "Thank you, Nina. His parents will be... There aren't words."

I am still in the doorway, one eye trained on the hallway. The sound of the gunshot—both gunshots—is still ringing in my ears, playing over and over like a snare drum stuck on one note. The Nazis will leave no stone unturned to find Talia. I must get her away from my parents or my father's dire predictions that I am placing them at far too much risk will come true.

"Come with me," I whisper, after a while. "Come and have a bath, let me get you some warm clothes. Are you hungry?"

She wrenches herself away from her sleeping student, and we walk down the hallway to my bedroom. "I'm not hungry," she whispers. "But I would love a bath."

I collect fresh fluffy towels from the rack in my bathroom. We hug briefly, and I close the door, the sound of water running, the most welcome thing I've heard all night.

And then, I go to sit at my dressing table. I stare at myself in the mirror for what feels like a long time. I need to get Talia and Mario away from here, yes, but before I do that, I need to ensure that Jack is not going to report her. I have to make him see sense.

And if I'm wrong, and I never knew him, and I don't know him now, then all we can do is run.

Half an hour later, Talia is asleep on my bed, tucked neatly into one side of the huge four-poster that my mother bought for my bedroom after I married Arturo. But I am standing by the window, staring down at the water, looking across at the silent domes of Santa Maria della Salute, as if they will give me the answers I need.

I fall asleep on my green silk sofa probably about four o'clock in the morning. I wake a few hours later, when I know that dawn will be washing a pink stain over the sky. I sit up, rubbing my eyes, but as I open them, all I can see are red stains, pooling across the dead Nazi's shirt.

And Jack, the sight of him standing there, our eyes locking in that way they have always done. But now I feel I don't know him at all.

Talia wakes to the scent of the coffee, fresh bread, and fruit that I have prepared for her breakfast. During the fitful hours of sleep that I had, Talia woke several times and murmured that she had killed a Nazi, grabbing my hand and talking half asleep. In the end, I soothed her by telling her that no one of consequence witnessed her.

Except Jack.

Talia raises herself on one elbow, and after she has stretched, woken properly, and gone to the bathroom, I sit on the edge of her bed.

"I don't want to appear ravenous," she says, "but I could murder this food."

"Eat as much as you like. Mario is still sleeping heavily."

She shakes her head, and a wry smile passes across her features. "You always know how to make things seem civilized, even when they are at their worst."

I slip off my shoes and climb onto the bed next to her while she eats. I love the way she tips her head back in appreciation at Papa's black-market coffee, the way she savors every bite of the warm bread.

"You have no idea how heavenly this is," she says.

"I think we all do, but some more than others." My voice is soft.

Her dark curls, freshly washed now, fall around her face, obscuring her expression.

We sit in silence for a while. It feels like everything is unsaid.

"Thank you for coming to Venice," she says finally. "Honestly, I hardly knew whether you would get my telegram." She lowers her voice. "How are things with Nico? And you must be so very worried about Raf."

I sigh. "I have not heard from Nico in three years," I say, honestly. "And I worry for Raf every day. He's fighting for the liberation of Rome, but you know..." I swipe a stray tear across my cheek. "There is no guarantee he'll come home safely." I swallow and change the topic. "Is there any news of your father?"

Talia places her coffee cup carefully back down. "Nothing. I think of him every day. Pray for him. At night, I try to imagine him safely in New York, with new patients, in an apartment. Surrounded by new friends."

I squeeze her hand. "Why didn't you leave with your father? I—"

Talia lowers her eyes. "I couldn't leave the children in my care, orphans, without protection, Jewish children, trapped in our city."

I close my eyes.

Talia continues. "There is something else you should know. Mario's parents are activists," she says, glancing at the closed, locked door. "Fedora and Lino Di Maggio are working with a resistance cell here in Venice. I stayed because they helped the children I was teaching to escape the city. We were working together, and had been carrying out this work for several months, so that was why I stayed."

"Oh, my darling Talia."

Talia nods and presses my hand tighter. "But now, they are high on the Nazis' wanted list. Mario's papers are false." She sighs. "*They were supposed to come* and find him after I fled. I couldn't risk dragging him across Venice to the church with me. Fedora was sending me messages as recently as the day of the new decree." She shakes her head. "But if they didn't... The Nazis are moving quickly."

I bite on my lip. "Yes."

She shudders. "Thank you, a thousand times, for rescuing him. I have no idea what went wrong, but I'm worried. Nina, they are Mario's family. I can't run away from Venice with him when he is not my child. I was only looking after him while they set up their new operation near the old arsenal. It was only for a few days. I... have to find out if they are alive or not. That poor child." She lowers her gaze. "I can't tell you how many other students of mine have lost their parents. Fedora helped three of my children escape through Italy to Spain. She is a true hero. On top of that, she's helped mothers who are stuck here in Venice when their husbands were taken away in September to escape. She took over after our head rabbi refused to give the Nazis the list of Jewish people in the city, and then committed suicide."

My eyes graze over her bird-like wrists, the pale skin on her arms.

She places the tray carefully on the side table next to the bed. "Nina, I need to know what's happened to them. I don't want to leave Venice without at least trying to get Mario back to them." She turns to look at me, her brown eyes with the golden hints unreadable. "I can't bear to see another child losing their parents. Teaching these children, I bonded with them. We've been through so much together, me trying to persuade them that what was happening in Germany would never happen here." She crosses her arms, clutching her shoulders. "They came in asking me so many questions. There were rumors of course, stories of horror that they had heard from their Jewish friends."

Talia's voice is tearful. "In the street, my students started being called 'Jew,' other children in the other neighborhoods of Venice yelling at them, as if their very identity was shameful. I saw the effects on them, how so many of them shrank inside themselves. Then, in September, when the disappearances started happening overnight, Fedora and I moved out as many families as we could." She lowers her gaze, her dark eyelashes sweeping her cheeks. "My neighborhood is empty. Our lives are gone, Nina. And I don't know whether we will ever get them back."

I rub my hands as if I am washing them. I see Talia glancing at me, and I stop.

Instead, in an effort to keep my hands still, I stand up and move across the room toward the window. "There is another problem."

"Jack."

"Do you remember his grandmother, Elisabetta Sabo? She lives in Dorsoduro. I wonder if he is staying with her." I pace around the room. "She and her husband used to run a fabric supply business. She supplied the silks and velvets for my mother's most beautiful gowns until recently when she retired. I want to go and speak to her, see if I can find out what he is really doing."

"He helped us, by dragging the body away."

"Did he? He is making it very clear that he is on the side of Hitler."

Talia frowns. "You are certain?"

I nod.

Her voice holds some of its old strength and conviction. "Well, then, Nina, you need to talk him around before we leave Venice. They're not going to stop until they find me."

"If he reports us."

"Yes," she says simply.

I lean heavily on my dressing table, staring at my middle-aged face in the mirror. I reach for my brush, drag it through my blond hair, the rhythmic movements soothing me. "I'll do everything I can to find out whether or not Mario's parents are alive. And today, I will go and see Elisabetta, and see what I can establish about Jack."

"We need to know what he's really up to. And preferably, we need him on our side." She whispers her last words. "How were you, seeing him again?"

I scrape a hand through my hair, tying it back into a neat little chignon. "Fine. It was over twenty years ago. Water under the bridge."

Through the mirror, Talia watches me.

CHAPTER 13

I leave Talia and Mario in my bedroom, catching up, and reading books together in my bed behind the locked door. Mario nearly fell over his own feet when he saw Talia, throwing himself into her arms and burying his head on her shoulder. I feel so much for them. Being with at least one of her students must go some way toward reassuring her that there were better times, that she had a rich life of her own before these tragic circumstances took over Europe. My sunglasses hide my darting eyes as I move closer to the old palazzo where I know Jack's grandmother, Elisabetta, still lives. The palazzo was abandoned by one of Venice's old aristocratic families at the end of the last century. A wealthy Roman businessman bought it and converted it into a series of charming and extremely expensive apartments. Elisabetta Sabo has lived here for decades. She was always lovely to me when I used to come and visit her with Jack.

Lost in my memories, I allow myself to dream a little as I walk across the Accademia Bridge. I wonder if the world will see such a joyous time as the 1920s ever again. Of course, it was followed by the economic devastation of the 1930s, and this, coupled with Germany's devastating losses after the Great War, have given rise to this horrendous situation under which we are all living.

I stop short, heavy footsteps are coming behind me. I turn cold, because the steps are not the soft treads of Italian leather shoes, nor are they the clip of women's high heels that one might expect in this wealthy part of Venice. No, my ears are attuned to this harsh beat. Anyone living in an occupied territory knows this sound and dreads it. The sound of jackboots collides with the thumping of my heart.

I fuss about with the shopping basket that I brought as a ruse. In it, I have placed a bunch of carrots, and some fresh green beans. I wait for the Nazi behind me to move on.

But he does not. I can sense him standing on the corner of the narrow lane that leads to the path that runs behind the great palazzos in this area, with their labyrinthine rooms tacked on over the centuries, as the families grew wealthier, and their need to display their riches increased accordingly.

I decide to turn my head and check to see who is following me.

My stomach caves. I grip the handle of my basket, and the carrots swoon dangerously inside.

It is the Nazi with the close-set blue eyes who waited for me outside Talia's house and harassed me as I tried to leave. I notice for the first time, his armband. It is decorated not only with a swastika on a red background, but with gold braid running across the top and the bottom. I know enough to recognize that the gold braid means he is a leader in the local area.

I rub my fingers together, making soothing patterns and telling myself to calm down. But I can't take my eyes off him, that sinister sneer, the piercing gaze.

Panicking, I turn around and walk back across the wooden Academia Bridge toward the Piazza San Marco from whence I came, making my way with resolution to the Café Florian, but the Nazi keeps pace behind me.

Inside the old café on the square, I settle myself into a private booth decorated with eighteenth-century paintings, and gaze out at the Piazza San Marco, trying to calm myself. The cathedral of San Marco looks the same as always, East meets West, a reminder of the exotic, rich history of Venice. I force myself to remember that this war is only a blip in time, but my heart pounds in my mouth. The Nazi has been seated by a waiter at one of the tables outside the café on the square.

I order the full Florian morning tea, spinach quiche, a selection of sandwiches. We can still procure fish in Venice, so I order some sandwiches with fish paste. I know that the English scones will be made with lard instead of butter, but the menu says they will still be served with local strawberry and apricot preserves.

The head waiter, Luciano, is a friend of my father's. I remind myself over and over that I am safe here.

But still, after an hour and a half, the Nazi has not budged. He has ordered an espresso, a silver platter of macaroons, and the newspaper, which he shakes with great fanfare in the sun, one leg snaked over the other.

I wonder if Jack's photograph is emblazoned across it today.

I call Luciano and ask him quietly to telephone my father. I say that I have accidentally ordered far too much food, and that I would like to invite Papa to join me. Fifteen minutes later, my father breezes in with a red cashmere scarf arranged neatly above his navy coat, and his tan shoes polished to a sheen. He shakes Luciano's hand firmly, asking him about the health of his wife.

The Nazi glances at them. I focus on Papa and the gray-haired Luciano.

"You see," Papa says, obligingly sitting down opposite me as if we do this every day and rubbing his hands together at the sight of the delicate white China plates of food, "this is where you prove to me that you are half English." He eyes the scones, jam, and cream. "You should have invited your mother; she would have been delighted."

"That would be a first."

Papa orders coffee and raises a brow.

I lean forward. The Nazi is well out of earshot, a strike against his skills in espionage. I keep my face neutral as I begin to speak. "I am being followed by the Nazi who stopped me outside Talia's house. He is at two o'clock. Man with the newspaper. Have decided he's a criminal in his other life." My eyes twinkle. I used to love playing this game with my father.

Father places his coffee cup down slowly. "Used to work in finance perhaps, and siphon off money for his own benefit. Nasty to his wife."

"She's relieved he's gone."

My father narrows his blue eyes. "He wasn't any use in Germany. The Nazis have sent him out here to get rid of him. Good riddance."

I chuckle. I place down the glass of champagne I have been sipping. "I wonder, would you consider it very rude if I were to go to the restroom?"

"I would be surprised if you didn't take the opportunity to escape."

"I'll take the back door; you keep an eye on the front."

Papa places his porcelain cup down in its saucer with great care. "If you go out the back door, you are admitting to something. Always take the front door if you can. But in this case, just this once, I quite agree with you. I shall walk straight past him when I exit, and if he asks me where you are, I shall say you are catching up with dear Luciano's wife in a private salon."

"Thank you," I say. "I have someone I need to meet. Much as I don't want to. If I disappear and don't come home, then you can ask—"

"The American." He speaks in a lower voice.

I glance around the café and make a split-second decision. "Talia is in my bedroom. I found her hiding in the roof of the San Danieli church."

"What?"

"She shot a member of the Gestapo who tried to murder the nun who was helping her when we were outside the church last night. Jack appeared to have been following us, and he took the body away. Obviously, I need to talk to him."

My father swivels a glance toward the Nazi. He clears his throat, the expression on his face giving nothing away. But the tone in his voice is low and dark when he speaks to me. "Don't trust him. The American. Until you are completely sure of his game."

"Jack's loyalty could go either way." I don't add that somewhere, deep inside, I'd be disappointed if his loyalty was only to himself.

I sense the Nazi's eyes on us. I feel them.

"Be careful, Evie," my father says simply. "And don't get involved if you have any doubts."

Oh, I'm already involved.

We both turn at the sight of a flurry outside in the square. The Nazi is demanding something of a waiter, becoming agitated, his face vivid red.

"Go," Papa whispers. "Now. And, Evie?"

I stand up carefully, leaving my coat hanging on the back of my chair.

"Don't break your own heart again."

Heat sweeps through my body, followed by ice. "I don't intend to."

My father nods at Luciano, and the tall, gray-haired waiter with the upright stance ushers me to the back of the restaurant, out the swinging door and through the labyrinth of kitchens, where the staff, consisting mostly of elderly men, stop and stare as I swish by, throwing my silk scarf over one shoulder. Luciano holds open the staff door for me without asking any questions at all. I hurry out into the cold Venetian air.

Don't break your own heart again.

I may not have a choice.

CHAPTER 14

I am flustered when I arrive at the back entrance to Jack's grandmother's palazzo in Dorsoduro. I have kept watch all around me the entire way here, but it seems Papa's ruse has worked, and I am alone for the first time since I stepped out of our house this morning. I beat down my fears of what the Nazi following me might mean for little Mario and Talia, and instead, I press the doorbell of apartment number twelve, out the back of the old palazzo whose front entrance seems to float on the Grand Canal.

I have so many treasured memories of my time here with Elisabetta and Jack. The first time he brought me here to meet her, I was nineteen, and entranced by her. I loved the close relationship she had with Jack, and quickly, she embraced and included me. Neither of them ever made me feel that I was anything but part of their little family. I swallow the lump that forms in my throat.

The door to the palazzo clicks open, and I climb the sweeping staircase to the top floor, my footsteps echoing on the stone stairs. I stand on the top landing to the side of the window and look down at the canal below. But there are no smart wooden boats holding my pursuer.

The door to apartment twelve is open, and Elisabetta, in her eighties now, is standing there. She is wearing a yellow silk blouse, with a pair of glasses hanging on a gold chain, waiting for me.

"*Bella Signora* Evelina," she says. "You have not aged a bit. Please, come in. I recognize you straight away. Of course, you are so like your mother. And she is a beautiful woman too."

"Signora Sabo," I say, leaning into her embrace. "*Come stai?* How are you?"

She places a powdery kiss firmly on my cheek, and holds me at arm's length a moment, her pretty eyes lighting up. "I am very well, thank you. Very well indeed."

I take in her neat, bobbed hair, tinted with a hint of elegant blond, her immaculate yellow silk blouse imprinted with tiny roses, the way it is tucked in perfectly to her black woolen skirt, the way she stands quite upright, making the most of her diminutive frame. "I hope you don't mind me saying that your blouse is most charming, Elisabetta."

"The blouse is Vianne Conti. Do you know of her?" She stands aside for me to come into the apartment.

"The girl from Paris who became a sensation on Fifth Avenue."

"*Si,*" she says, her voice rich and warm.

We come into Elisabetta's salon, decorated with raspberry velvet sofas, chandeliers, a grand piano heaving with framed silver photographs.

Elisabetta rings an old-fashioned bell pull. An elderly housekeeper appears, and Elisabetta asks for coffee and tells me to sit down.

"You remember, bella Evelina? I used to own a fabric supply business," she says wistfully, settling herself on the sofa opposite me, perfectly upright, and crossing her slim legs at the ankles. "With my husband. He was a wonderful man."

I bite on my lip. I had forgotten how lovely and open Elisabetta is. I need to direct the conversation, but it was always hopeless, when it came to Elisabetta, I remember with a slightly sinking heart.

She is miles away. "We had shops in Venice, Milano, and Rome. My family is a comfort; I have three sons and eight grandchildren," she goes on, talking in a low, urgent voice. "Every Christmas, we used to gather here in Venice, do you remember that, and they would all come to see me from America, Rome, Paris... It was wonderful."

I realize with a pang that I don't know whether or not Jack is married. I glance at the silver-framed photos on the grand piano, but I am not close enough to see features and faces clearly.

Elisabetta eyes me. Her gaze is warm, but there is an astuteness there that I recognize in a fellow businesswoman. I remind myself that is who I am now, too.

"Jack's father went to New York after the last war and fell in love with an American woman. It took me a long time to accept that he wasn't coming home to Venice. But my son always brought his family out to Italy for Christmas every year. We had a wonderful time. Jack is a journalist, his brother is an engineer," she starts counting off on her fingers, "and Jack's youngest brother teaches advanced mathematics at Stanford University. That one cooks very well too. That is the Italian in him. But for the fifth Christmas in a row, we will not be together." She tuts and shakes her head.

I nod and make sympathetic noises.

"My late husband and I used to supply the major fashion houses all over the world with lace and the finest silks, do you remember? We also supplied individual clients who only had their dresses made up by the very best dressmakers in Europe.

Brides, women who were going to fashionable events, the opera. I would travel all over Europe and the Orient to purchase the fabrics, and then, you see, they were so precious to me, so fine as they slipped through my fingers, that I would not sell them to just anyone. Once, I looked at a bride-to-be and decided that I could not part with a certain beautiful lace, because I was sure she was not in love with the man she was going to marry!"

I stifle a smile.

"No, I would match the fabric with the customer. I would decide whether or not they were worthy of my lovely pieces. Vianne Conti is lovely, just like you," Elisabetta says, switching tack suddenly. "I would have given you any exquisite lace, white velvet or silk that you desired, Evelina. I was so saddened when you and Jack parted, my dear."

I open my mouth, but Elisabetta continues.

"Vianne Conti is one of my favorite people. I would always bring out my most special silks for her. She deserved them. And where is your husband, bella?" she asks, suddenly. "I assume a charming woman like you is married, no?"

The housekeeper brings coffee, and I offer to pour. "My husband died seven years ago," I say. "He was young."

"Oh, I am sorry, *bella.*" Elisabetta shakes her head. "I was lucky that my late husband only died two years ago. We were married for sixty-two years." She smiles at me, and I feel my shoulders soften. I allow myself to relax a little. Elisabetta's apartment feels like it is a world away from Nazis, but I have to move forward. I feel a twinge of guilt that I'm about to exploit her hospitality, but if she knew why I was doing so, surely, she might understand. I think of Talia and Mario hiding away in my bedroom at the palazzo, and reality comes back to me again. "Would you mind very much if I used your powder room?"

"But of course. Jack is at the radio station. I take it you two have met again. Although, I am delighted for you to visit me for any reason at all." She rubs her hands together. "He is carrying out his daily broadcast back to New York." Elisabetta visibly puffs up a little with pride. She looks at the wireless that sits beneath the enormous window that overlooks the Grand Canal. "It starts in five minutes. Shall we listen to it together?"

"That's a good idea," I say.

She gives me directions to the bathroom, through a door that leads directly out of the salon, down the hallway, and I will find it through the last door on the right. I close my eyes with thanks that I am being directed through a different door than the one the housekeeper left through.

I slip away and close the door softly behind me.

Wood-paneled walls lined with paintings of Venice, soft carpets, Murano glass chandeliers, hallway tables with lamps. Six doors, three running off each side of the hallway. I take off my shoes, and as silently as possible, pop my head into each room. Another small sitting room, a bedroom decorated all in pale pink silk, Elisabetta's. A room with a dark wooden desk, the drapes drawn and an air of sadness. Her late husband's study.

A bedroom decorated in cream and beige. A shirt hanging on the outside of the wardrobe. A pair of men's shoes placed underneath the window. *Bingo.* I slip inside. My heart races at the sight of the stack of books by the bed. The reading glasses, a telltale sign of age, the silk dressing gown draped neatly on a cream velvet chaise longue all make my heart skip around again. Jack would be furious if he found out what I'm about to do. But I need to know whose side he is on. Talia's life will be in danger otherwise.

As I look around, I can't help feeling drawn to these intricate details and intimacy that I never had the chance to know about Jack.

I stamp down my strange feelings of regret and nostalgia and go straight to the bed, and search underneath it. Nothing.

The bedside drawers contain only a spare wallet, which is empty, a set of keys, a few bookmarks.

I open the armoire. Check the pockets of his well-cut suits. Flick my fingers through the rows of pristine shirts. Dislodge the polished leather shoes. Check for any hidden panels in the wood, but still there is nothing. I am beginning to doubt that there is anything to find. Perhaps he is not doing anything untoward. A weight lifts from my shoulders at this point.

There is a bathroom leading directly from his bedroom. I raise a brow at the stunning black Carrera marble from floor to ceiling. I scour the cupboards and check my watch. I don't want to miss the broadcast and I do not want to be caught red-handed by Elisabetta. Again, the bathroom cupboards are immaculate and only contain men's aftershave, spritzes and toothpaste, the necessary adages.

At this rate, I will have to strip the bed.

Darned Jack.

Heat pricks my cheeks, as I go back to the bedroom, get down on my hands and knees and run my fingers over the entire bedroom floor. And that is when I find it. A cut in the floorboards.

I pull the pocketknife that I always carry these days out of the lining of my handbag. Prize open the floorboards.

And there it is. A spy suitcase radio and a headset.

I shake my head. He could be working for the Nazis, reporting for them. I carefully, quietly, click open the suitcase. Inside, there is a full spy radio, a listening station which would have the ability to pick up codes and send them overseas. And tucked beneath is a leaflet from America setting out Morse code.

I sit back. Immeasurably relieved.

It is one of the most dangerous roles there is during the war.

Radio operators in England are being parachuted into France to report back home on the occupation. They are warned that their projected lifespan is, on average, six weeks.

My hands remain steady as I carefully place Jack's equipment back and clip the radio suitcase closed. I secure the floor, stand up, run my eyes over his room one last time to ensure everything is exactly as I found it, and step back out to the hallway, find the bathroom, flush the lavatory, wash my hands, and run the faucet. I am convinced Jack has nothing to do with the Nazis, but while I expected only relief, I worry for him, for what he's got himself into, and what it means that he dragged that Nazi body away.

I walk back out to Elisabetta. A tiny dog has appeared and is sitting at her heels. She offers it a piece of biscuit.

"Would you like me to turn on the wireless now?" I ask.

"Please." She pats the dog and chats to it.

I settle down in the seat nearest to her, and we wait for Jack's broadcast to begin.

"This is the American station," Elisabetta says, smiling proudly. "Jack has set up an aerial so that I can receive it and listen to him twice a week. He is a wonderful journalist. I am enormously proud of my grandchildren... The ones in Rome have—"

Jack's voice burns into the room and his grandmother brings her own hand to her mouth to silence herself.

He speaks rapidly in Italian for about ten minutes, reporting the news from Italy in a neutral, formal register, not incriminating the Nazis, just stating the facts. He reports on the outcome of the Verona Convention two days ago and sets out the new rules for Jewish citizens here. He is formal, precise, to the point.

I pour myself another espresso; the coffee is good after my sleepless night, and I offer it to Elisabetta, but she shakes her head, glued to the wireless, to her grandson, to this link with the family she clearly adores.

I sip the coffee and then stop, the cup poised.

Jack is speaking in English. Elisabetta smiles and returns to petting the dog, clearly not understanding what he's saying, nor showing any interest. As far as she is concerned, he is probably just translating what he's already said. But my pulse quickens. For ten full minutes, he talks utter gibberish; words messed up, sentences jumbled. It is code.

I go and stand by the wireless, frowning. None of it makes an iota of sense.

Once the broadcast is finished, I turn the wireless off. I can feel my cheeks flushing. None of this makes an iota of sense.

"Very good," Elisabetta says, "isn't he?"

"Oh, he's good," I say.

Jack comes into Elisabetta's apartment a little later, his tie loose, the top button of his shirt undone. His eyes search mine, and he glances at his grandmother.

"I have things to do," she announces. "I shall leave you two alone." She stands up, pats down her outfit, and disappears through the door into the hallway.

Jack glances around the room as if looking for someone. "It is not safe for you to be here, Lina."

"To be safe, I would have remained in Tuscany. I want you to talk to me, Jack."

He sits down opposite me, leans forward, clasping his hands between his knees. "It's a mistake you being here." He sighs heavily.

I shrug. "It was always a mistake, Jack."

His eyes tilt up toward me, the green in them flashing, and the dint in his chin deepens. "What can I do?"

"Tell me the truth."

He frowns and goes to the drinks cabinet, leaning against it and facing me.

I continue speaking. "I am glad to see you are discreet. I trust that discretion extends to old friends."

He stands up, rubs a hand through his hair, and comes over

to sit down right next to me, and my insides start zapping, as if every fiber of my being is alive, small electric darts shooting through me, hitting my nerve ends.

"Why do you think I came back to Venice, Lina?" he murmurs.

I tip my head back, and I sense him looking up at me, sense those eyes seeing through every fiber of my being.

"For a start, you need to move Talia and the child away from your parents," he says. "It's not safe for them there."

I take in a sharp breath. "My parents have changed, Jack. But have you?"

Front entrance hall, pink traveling costume. Luggage packed, white gloves, pillbox hat. My mother, glorious in a carmine dress, standing on the staircase, eyeing us like we are children who have run away from school. "What on earth do you think you're doing?"

Going to New York with Jack. My twenty-year-old eyes glitch and can't look at her.

Next to me, Jack extracts his hand from mine. It's not the first time I doubt him, but I push on, wanting to believe that he cares for me more than my parents do, that he sees me as a person, not as a vehicle for his own gain.

But now he's taken a step away from me. I can hear his breathing, and I can almost see the disdain curling from my mother's lips.

"Go home, Mr. Sabo. How could you possibly think that I would ever entertain the idea of my daughter marrying a news-paper man? Evelina, go to your room. And don't come out until I've dealt with this."

I begin to protest, to explain, until I turn in shock and confusion as Jack simply bows his head and walks away, out the door, leaving the palazzo. I stand there, alone in the entrance hall, pain piercing my insides, my heart shrinking as the life I thought I was going to lead disappears before my eyes.

"No!" I say, firmly, but I'm talking to Jack's retreating back. He's already only a shape visible through the open front door, retreating toward the water taxi that was going to be our escape. "Jack?" I frown, throw my suitcase down on the ground, but my mother restrains my arm.

"He's walking away," she murmurs, her voice like snowflakes falling onto warm sand. "Don't appear desperate, Evelina."

"Excuse me," I say, wrenching my arm away from her.

She lets go. "Better he leaves now than in ten years' time when you are poor and alone in a foreign country with children. Let him go."

"What?" I shake my head and run out the door.

But he's in the water taxi. The engine fires up. I wave my hands in the air, but they flutter about, as if they have lost track of what they should be doing.

He won't look at me. The taxi starts to move.

I grip my elbows, my arms, anything. "No," I whisper. The years stretch ahead of me and the story I've written for myself, sweeping romance, New York, Jack coming home at night to a sweet apartment in a brownstone in Brooklyn, falls away like droplets of rain into the canal, disappearing and merging into a great pool of loss.

It's overwhelming. I love him. But I stand on the dock outside my parents' home and watch him go, and a feeling of hopelessness washes over me.

He is behaving like a child. Scared of my mother.

And he didn't think it was worth fighting for me.

It's a strange kind of disappointment, marked by the physical distance between us that means I never really understand why he told me he wanted to spend the rest of his life with me, but ran away and didn't fight.

I've fought ever since then. Been determined not to accept things that I don't like. Been determined never to let anyone down in the way Jack let me down, because I know how much it hurt.

"Do people change?"

I laugh. "Do they become braver, Jack? It wasn't me who walked away. I never would have."

He leans back on the sofa, stretches his arms behind his head, sighs heavily.

I stand up, wander across the room, suddenly overheated. "I searched your room."

"Of course you did."

A smile dances on my lips and he stands up, comes over to me. "You are being followed."

"I'm aware," I say.

"So, bring them here. Elisabetta and I will hide them."

His voice is so low, so soft and my thoughts freeze, only to spring back to life.

"The thing is, I don't know who I can trust." My voice is hardly a whisper.

"You can trust me," he murmurs. "Always. Lina, bring Talia and the child here to Elisabetta and I. They are not safe at the palazzo. You are putting your parents, you, and them at too much risk. I'll help you bring them here in the cover of darkness tonight. The Nazis will never suspect me."

I close my eyes, feeling sweat beading on my upper lip. He's right, but I still don't know if I can trust him, if he too has really changed. But at this point, what other choice do I have?

CHAPTER 15

That evening, we make the journey to Elisabetta's house; Jack and I walking Talia and Mario separately. I hope my presence in recent days has reassured Mario that he is safe with us. Deftly, we leave the palazzo out the back way during the changeover in the Nazi guard's routine. At Elisabetta's house, she bustles about, pulling out a saucepan of vegetable broth from the small refrigerator, and a large knob of bread. Jack has to return to the radio station. My eyes flash against his, but he picks up his coat. Elisabetta is unbothered. A tension simmers away within me. Talia stands silently, her hands in the pocket of her coat where she keeps her gun.

"Elisabetta," I protest, turning my attention toward the elderly woman stirring the large saucepan on the stove. "Surely these are your rations for the next week?"

"Jack will obtain more food." She eyes me and opens a cupboard. It is stocked with flour, eggs, and there is powdered milk, a bunch of broccoli. Carrots and oranges. It seems that Jack's connections, whatever they are, are at least beneficial when it comes to the supply of food.

Elisabetta lights the stovetop, and soon the kitchen is filled with the rich scent of her broth cooking. She slices the bread, and butters it.

"The Nazis turn the power on only in the evening so that we can cook, and not until eight o'clock." She raises her eyes to the roof. "They think this is a punishment, because they assume we all eat like infants at six o'clock as the Germans do, and they hope that in restricting the hours of our power supply that we will freeze and starve. But they underestimated the Italians' ability to wait. We do not run our lives by the clock. Please, have a piece of bread," she says, offering me the plate. "You must be exhausted. And I want you to tell me what is going on," she asks me, matter-of-factly.

"No, I am fine." I take in a deep breath and frown at the closed door that Jack has disappeared through.

"Are you quite all right?" Elisabetta asks.

"Sì," I say. A lump the size of a ping-pong ball forms in my throat.

She nods, but eyes me as if she knows I'm not telling the entire story. "I am pleased that the nuns were helping. They can be extraordinary women," she says.

I realize Jack must have told her about Talia.

Elisabetta takes the wooden spoon from the now bubbling pan of vegetable soup and lays it down carefully on a plate on the kitchen bench. "I am more than happy to help, Evelina. I had... *have* wonderful Jewish friends. My husband and I used to go on vacation with a dear couple who owned the shop next door to ours just around the corner from here." Her voice falters. "They were rounded up in September as soon as the Nazis arrived in Venice and taken away before they had time to gather themselves, or even think about getting away from Venice. I have tried... I have asked Jack to try to find out what their fate has been, but he hears nothing."

"It is the silence that is awful," I say.

Elisabetta nods. "I'm only helping in a ridiculously small

way. It is the least I can do. Having your friends here takes my mind off worrying about the fate of my own Jewish friends. I am not sleeping, you see. But this way, at least I am doing something."

"I am sorry. There are not words. But, as I say, I don't want to put you at any further risk. I have a couple of things I need to do here in Venice, and then we will go."

Elisabetta sighs heavily. "I am eighty-three years old, Evelina. I have lived a full life, and I am not scared of the Germans at this point. It is more important to me to help."

She turns back to her soup.

By the time Talia and Mario emerge, their hair freshly washed and combed, dressed in an assortment of oversized dressing gowns, sweaters, and pajamas that Elisabetta took from Jack's room, the table is set with two bowls of vegetable broth, three servings of bread, three glasses of milk, powdered. Talia watches before eating her own food and tries to remind Mario not to gulp it all down.

I stand back in the kitchen with Elisabetta, my eyes on Talia. Her hands are scabbed, and they shake as she manages a few sips of soup with her spoon.

Mario finishes his meal, pushes his plate away, and chatters with Elisabetta. It is a credit to Talia that he is not afraid of Elisabetta and I. He tells Elisabetta that he used to be naughty at school, but now he is trying to be good so that his friends will come back. He lists off a series of boys' names.

I close my eyes.

When Talia finishes and thanks Elisabetta, the elderly woman eyes her and insists that they go to bed and rest, turning down Talia's offers of assistance cleaning up. I stay in the kitchen and help, finding the gentle actions of washing dishes and drying them only a small distraction to the worry I have.

.   .   .

Later, Elisabetta goes to bed, and Talia is asleep. Outside, all is quiet in the late Venetian night. My ears are pricked for the sound of Jack. I feel an insatiable urge to glance down through the kitchen window, pulling aside the blackout blinds in the kitchen to check there is nobody standing in the narrow lane below, but for what feels like hours, I sit in the darkened sitting room waiting for him while the rest of the household sleeps.

As time passes, I become attuned to the sounds around me, the rhythmic creaking of the wind against the windowpane. The wristwatch that Arturo gave me for our tenth wedding anniversary tells me it is ten o'clock when a set of footsteps sounds outside on the cobblestones.

Who is it?

The door opens. I hold my breath, taking in the figure of a man, tall, imposing, until he steps into the room and I see it is Jack. My heartbeat returns to normal. He moves across the room to the drinks cabinet when he comes in, scowling, and tapping his foot on the floor while he pours himself a tumbler of brandy.

"I am going to make a report back to the States tonight," he says, tipping his head back and swallowing the drink.

"What do they do with the news you send back to New York? What, if anything are they doing about the reports of this dreadful camp in Poland? If we are to believe the BBC, they report that the Nazis are shooting elderly Jewish people on arrival."

"I think the world's heart will collectively break for a very long time." He looks at me helplessly. "I'm not sure that there is much they can do, Lina. Can we change the topic? How are you?"

I feel a sharp little intake of breath and look away from him.

"Have you been happy?" he asks.

I tip my head back. "Of course."

Who knows, he probably has a wife and children back in

THE VENETIAN DAUGHTER 115

New York. A brownstone in Brooklyn, a steady job at a newspaper or radio station to return to. I gather myself and turn back to him.

He looks down at Elisabetta's sofa, trails a hand across its back. Jack opens his mouth as if he is about to say something, but then thinks better of it, and closes it again. Eventually, he speaks.

"I never married." He is not looking at me, but I feel his every word as if it were my own. "I've spent the last twenty years as a foreign correspondent roaming around Europe and South America. I've never settled down." He lets out a sad laugh. "I seem to need to move every couple of years for some reason. I'm not sure what I'm looking for, to be honest. And then, when the opportunity came up to report back from Venice, I grabbed it. Elisabetta... and perhaps, finally, the chance to be near you. I knew things were going to be awful for Talia, too."

I fold my hands on my lap and bite my lower lip.

"Tell me honestly, have you been happy, Lina? Did it all turn out as your mother planned?"

I stand up, move toward the wireless from which his grandmother listens to his broadcasts and his secret codes so loyally every day. "I have been fortunate," I say, not wanting to be disloyal to Arturo, to the love we shared, to the family we built together, or tried to build. "I am grateful for what I have, so yes, I have been content." I don't tell him that Arturo is dead. Or about who Nico has become. For some reason, the words won't come to my lips.

He looks at me, for one long searing moment. "We should get some sleep, Lina." He holds the door open. "You can sleep in my bed. I'll take the sofa out here and keep watch. Goodnight, Lina. Get some rest."

I simply nod at him. He moves back toward the sofa, and I, in turn, walk away.

CHAPTER 16

I sleep until dawn in Jack's bed. But when I wake, my thoughts fly in all directions—panic, anger, fear for Elisabetta and the danger we have put her in, worry as to what the next steps are for Talia and Mario, and while I feel overwhelmed with all these concerns, one aching sadness eclipses everything.

My sadness for the total lack of compassion the Germans have for others, for innocent civilians, for teachers and grandmothers and for children who are just trying to grow up. It seems to me that when empathy leaves a community, then that is the end.

I'm haunted by what I saw in Talia's *sestiere*, terrified that she has killed a Nazi and will be caught, confused, and heightened and so darned unsure about the fact that I'm relying on Jack.

As the hours crack on, and I remain impossibly awake, one thing becomes perfectly clear. I must get Talia out of Venice, find Mario's parents, and get them both to safety as quickly as possible.

I worry too about Elisabetta, my thoughts plagued by the recent massacre at the border town of Boves, when 350 Italian civilians were brutally murdered. The majority of the victims of the terrible massacre were elderly or infirm, after locals in the town near the French border rebelled and took two Nazi soldiers captive. One of the captive soldiers was killed in the skirmish when the Germans tried to rescue him. The massacre of the remaining citizens of Boves was in reprisal for the death of that one Nazi soldier.

As an act of ultimate revenge, the Italian town was then burned to the ground. We all knew this was done as a warning to the rest of us. A warning that the terrible fantasy that is playing out in Europe is no imagined story. It is real. The reports that came out were horrific. One of the most poignant was that of an elderly Italian woman who was bedridden and was burned to death by the Nazis in her own bedroom. She was in her eighties. Elisabetta, also in her eighties, is sleeping in the next room to mine. While it is vital that I get Talia out of Venice, what happened in Boves has highlighted that I can't accept Elisabetta's hospitality for very long.

My thoughts turn darker. If the Nazis work out that Talia had anything to do with the death of that Nazi last night, they will hunt her down and murder her. What's worse, the implications could be dire for Venice, for this entire *sestiere*.

I place my head in my hands.

Elisabetta, my parents, all the villagers who trust me in Tuscany, my two sons—will they end up like the 350 people massacred with no mercy in Boves. Whom, out of all those that I care about do I put at risk because I cannot lose my darling friend?

Soon, Mario calls out. I go to his bedroom door and pat the whimpering child back to sleep as if he were one of my babies.

He is someone else's baby. And I need to find his parents. I look at the curve of his small arm resting in front of his face. If someone else was caring for my child in my absence, then I would hope they would do whatever it took to keep them safe.

A faint hint of healthy blush appears on the sleeping child's cheek.

"Goodness knows I shall take care of you, *mio caro*," I whisper to the child.

In his half slumber, he reaches out and places his soft little hand over mine.

Elisabetta is busy in the kitchen with Talia. Jack has gone down to the radio station and Mario is eating an orange, drinking milk out of a blue-and-white mug. Talia and I play with Mario after breakfast, presenting him with some of Elisabetta's grandchildren's puzzles and wooden toys. Elisabetta supervises from the comfort of her sofa, but I find myself focusing on the closed and curtained window that looks over the laneway outside, yearning to go and stand there and keep watch.

Jack arrives home mid-morning. When his key turns in the door, Talia and I share a glance.

And when he comes in carrying a cardboard box with carrot tops sticking out of it, I feel her gratitude as much as my own.

"Good morning," Elisabetta says. "*Grazie mille*, Jack. That is just the thing. Vegetables."

"Good morning, Nonna," he says, patting Mario on his head. "Lina, would you come and talk with me for a moment in my grandfather's office?"

I send Elisabetta a glance, and she waves me on.

Jack holds the door open for me to go up the hallway of the apartment to his late grandfather's study.

We enter and he presses his hand to his temple.

"I'm not going to beat about the bush. The death of the Nazi has been discovered. It will be reported in the newspapers tonight and the murderer is being hunted, with calls for a ransom if he is turned in."

I lean heavily against the back of Jack's grandfather's leather chair. There is a gold clock on the mantelpiece. I notice it for the first time, and its tick seems to take on more meaning than ever before. "How much do they know?"

Jack shakes his head. "They do know that the man was covering the *sestiere* of San Polo. The SS have started questioning residents around the church. I hope there were no witnesses, but the reality is that we were in an open square, Lina."

I nod but stay quiet.

"I don't know whether the residents of the square were protecting the nuns and knew what was going on, or not."

I shake my head. "We need to move them away from Elisabetta, in case someone did see you and they come here," I whisper, terrified for Elisabetta.

He scowls at his father's desk. "But your parents' house remains under surveillance, Lina." Jack shakes his head. "I went by this morning."

I jump at the sound of Mario calling out to Talia.

"Don't worry. The Nazi did not see me. But..." Jack sits down on one of the leather chairs. He indicates that I sit down on the other one, so we both perch, facing the desk. "I did hear some other news."

I turn to him.

"Prepare yourself," he says.

"What more could there possibly be, Jack?"

Jack's brow furrows, and he lowers his voice. "Apparently your son, Nico, arrived back in Venice last night. One of the people at the station went to school with him and reported his return. They also mentioned that he is running a Nazi ammunition factory in Milano."

A mixture of emotions swells through me. I will see him. Talk to him, make him—no, help him—see sense. Bring him home to me... Then the old questions come gnawing at me. *How did I fail as a mother? What is he doing here?*

"The Nazis know him and admire him," Jack says matter-of-factly.

Tears well on the edges of my eyes and threaten to trail down my cheeks, but resolutely, I talk. "I have two sons, Jack. My youngest, Raf, is stationed in southern Italy, and Nico... I cannot abide what he is doing."

"You cannot choose what your adult children do." Jack is beside me, holding my hands.

I close my eyes. "It is my fault. After his father died, I..."

I feel Jack tensing, but I continue, not wanting to linger for now.

"After Arturo's death, I took over the family businesses, and I did my best." I open my eyes and raise my head to meet his gaze. "I have so many people relying on me, you see. But while I was taking care of everyone else, I lost my son. I let his grief slip through my fingers, and I lost him, somehow. But I had to keep everything going."

Jack leans closer to me. He sends a glance toward the door. "How deep does Nico's loyalty to the Nazis really run? This is a question that I hate to ask, but would he betray his own mother?"

"What are you asking me, Jack?"

"Would your father tell him about Talia and trust him?" He pauses. "I have to ask you: do you think your son is dangerous?"

The room is silent, save from the ticking of his grandfather's golden clock.

"Of course not," I whisper, with more resolution than I feel.

CHAPTER 17

Jack insists on coming with me to my family's palazzo once the sun is fully up in the sky. We stick close to each other as I lead us home on instinct. When we come to the back entrance, we hide. But there is no Nazi standing guard, and after a while, we move forward, only to come to a stop. There are voices coming from the garden inside the boundary wall. They are speaking German. One of them is the blue-eyed Nazi's voice. I recognize it as it seems to be imprinted in my memory.

The other voice is one that I would know anywhere. My heart sinks, and I close my eyes. It belongs to my eldest son.

"Lina," Jack whispers and catches me when I almost trip over at the edge of the alleyway. Anger, guilt, sadness and wretched tears are all fighting for first place in my heart and mind. Clear as day, the voices belong to the Nazi and Nico. They are laughing! I fight down the bile that wants to course up my throat.

Jack pulls me into the shelter of a small park.

"Lina, can you keep moving?" He lowers his voice even further, holding me close. "Would you like to get some coffee? Can you make it around the corner?"

I close my eyes to steady the colors and the pulsating noises in my ears. "I am sorry. This is..."

"Don't apologize. Never, to me."

Would Nico have turned out like this if Arturo had lived? How am I supposed to look after Talia and Mario, when I'm not capable of raising my own?

All my instincts tell me to go back to the palazzo and speak to my confused, misguided son, but he is with a Nazi. Clearly enjoying himself. As a mother, I want to talk to him, sit down with him and explain what he is doing. All those young men who have lost their lives in the name of war, and my son is profiteering instead. I bow my head in shame. Thank goodness we got Talia and Mario out before he arrived.

Overhearing Nico and the Nazi comes on top of the dreadful news that I heard on the BBC this morning, doubling down on what feels like an impossible situation. The British have called off the American assault on the Bernhardt Line here in Italy, following heavy casualties from the fierce German resistance, and the Japanese have sunk an American submarine in the South Pacific.

And, as if on cue, the air around us, and the ground beneath our feet begins to rumble ominously.

A formation of aircraft fly over Venice. Jack and I stand in silence, waiting until the din dies down. We shade our eyes and look upward and when we do, we see the dreaded swastika painted on the side of the planes.

Jack turns to me once the aircraft have gone. "Lina, the war is going to go on regardless of what Nico chooses to do. I know it's going to be difficult, but you must push what he is doing aside, and focus on what you can achieve. So far, you have searched for Talia, found her, and Mario. They are both alive and safe. You cannot choose what Nico decides to do. He is a grown man. You must let go."

I shake my head, as the aircraft disappear into the distance, no doubt flying up north, perhaps back to Germany after carrying out a bombing raid over Rome. "You are right, we can only choose our own actions, not those of others. I know that." I search his face, and he smiles at me. "But you must understand, I brought him into the world. I feel responsible for my family. War destroys families in multiple ways," I say, shuddering. "Jack, I'm going to walk back home now, and talk to my son." I turn to look at the way back to my childhood home. "And what I truly hope is that I can connect with him."

I turn back to face Jack, and we share a long look. I only hope that a mother's love will bring my son back to me.

When I step through the gate into my parents' garden, Nico is standing outside, alone. I send up a prayer of thanks that the German appears to have gone.

I close the back gate to the garden softly behind me.

"Nico." I hesitate, unsure whether to move toward him.

"Hello, Mama," he says. He looks at me with that earnestness in his eyes that I remember from when he was little, and I stop for a moment, allowing relief to wash over me.

"How are you?" I ask my son, the polite question forming on my lips when I have no other words to say. The intense feelings I had after his initial greeting are replaced by trepidation, and ball bearings start tumbling around in my gut.

"I am well," he replies. His blue eyes flicker, and his short blond hair glimmers in the sunlight. I beat back the terrifying thought that he is exactly what the Nazis want in a young man.

"Nico... I love you," I say. I know this conversation is going to be difficult, but I must let him know that he is safe with me. I worry that that is what this is all about, him flailing about and trying to find security in a world that feels as if it is falling apart. He changed so much after Arturo died. He was trying to become a man, but has attached himself to an unstable rock, in wanting to find something to hold on to.

His eyes flicker, but he does not respond to me immediately.

"Mama," he murmurs eventually. "I am sorry about what happened between us. I was angry, reckless. I should never have shouted at you."

Again, relief spreads through me. My shoulders soften. This is the Nico I know.

"And I am sorry too," I say. I still have a long way to go.

"But we need to talk," I say.

Nico holds the door to the palazzo open for me and we walk in silence through the grand entrance hall.

Papa's sitting room is empty, but there is a fire crackling cheerfully in the grate.

We sit down awkwardly, both of us hovering on the edge of Papa's velvet sofa.

"Darling, tell me what is going on."

"There are things I cannot talk of," Nico says.

I take a breath. "Nico," I manage. "Remember, friendship and love are worth far more than money and business." It sounds obvious, and yet the silence in the room could be broken by the drop of a pin.

He glances at the diamonds on my fingers.

I shake my head. "Come home and help me run the estates," I whisper. "We are feeding refugees, taking care of the tenant farmers. Cara, Alphonso, Bettina and I are doing everything we can, but we would welcome you with open arms. We would value you."

He stands up, goes to the fireplace, and leans against it, facing away from me as he stares down at the flames. I can see the tension in his shoulders, the rigidity, markers of the strong anger he showed toward me that dreadful day when we last spoke. My stomach tightens again in response.

"You are being followed, Mama."

"Yes."

"You are on a list of suspects." He turns around and faces me. "The Nazi who has been following you is named Otto

Ablenz. He is odd, yes, but he is ruthless. You must not under-estimate the fact that he is stalking you. He knows that you took the Jewish child from Talia Baruch's house, knows that you are protecting him. They... Please, Mama. Don't take any more risks. I can't lose you too..." He falters on the last words, as he stands there, his hands hanging at his sides. He is wearing the signet ring his father gave him for his eighteenth birthday. "You are taking risks that you know are dangerous. You have been putting the whole family at risk, my grandparents, their home..." He shakes his head. "Otto Ablenz is a trained killer, and he is after you." He walks back over to the sofa and sits next to me. "You are being naïve. You need to be far more careful than this."

I tip my head back and close my eyes. "Nico."

He swings around to face me. And I know it. I know that all he wants is to be supported. To feel secure. To know that I care, that I love him, and that I would never let him down. But grief hit me like a ton of bricks after his father died, and I was grieving too, while Raf, bless him, seemed to cope with the loss of his father far better than Nico or me. I know that my eldest son is still struggling with the loss.

"Remember how I told you that if I could have done, I would have made Talia your godmother? That because she was of the Jewish faith, she could not be godmother to you, but I told you in spirit that she was like a second mother to you. An honorary godmother. And you knew it too. You loved her so much."

A muscle in his cheek twitches. He opens and closes his hands by his side. "Yes, I know. I love Talia."

"Nico, you must know how dangerous the war is for Talia. You know that she and I have been friends since I was six years old. She has been by my side through everything. She came to us after your papa died. She looked after us all, and quite frankly, if she had not done that, I don't know what sort of state

I would be in. If I had one wish in the world, it would be for you to have a friend like Talia. I would want that for everyone."

He is silent.

"As you get older, you come to realize that friendship is everything. Friendship, and love, Nico. I love you both, you and Talia. But you need to think about the impact of all this on her."

His blond eyebrows crease into a frown. "I know how much she means to you, but I can't control the policies that we live under."

"No, but you can maintain silence and protect her and her young student."

"What do you think I'm going to do? Turn them into the Nazis? You honestly think I am as bad as this?"

I take in a shaking breath. His anger is back now. "I know you'd never do that."

His mouth turns up in a strange smile. "I will never betray Talia. I promise you that, Mama."

I sink back on the sofa. "I believe you. I honestly do. But you need to remember that you have the power to make choices, and those choices have an impact. Trust yourself, Nico, trust your instincts. You are loved, and your father is watching over you."

He wipes a hand across his forehead. "I don't know whether he is," he murmurs. "I just don't feel him around... I don't think he would be proud of me."

My heart contracts. "Just think of Talia, and that little boy. That is what your father would want you to do."

Nico averts his gaze. He stands, unnaturally still. "Maybe. I don't agree with you on all things when it comes to this war and what we should be doing to provide and protect our family's future, but on Talia, I do. She is safe?"

I need to believe that I can trust him. My own son. I refuse to consider anything else and to repair our relationship, I need to be able to be open with him. To trust him as any mother would want to trust her own son. Trust in him will go a long way toward fixing this. My mother doesn't trust my decisions, still disapproves of the fact I haven't rushed into another marriage.

I lean forward, my decision made, and speak. My relationship with my son is one of the most important things in the world to me. "I have her. She is with me. I will always ensure she is safe."

Nico nods. "Good," he whispers.

"I want you to promise me that you will remember how much she loves you, and how much she trusts our family. Trusts you."

Finally, he nods. "I know," he says quietly. "But I worry about you."

"And you, Mama."

I sink back on the sofa and close my eyes. I've done it. I've got through to him. I exhale and let the relief wash over me.

CHAPTER 18

Rain pelts over Venice as soon as darkness falls. It had been threatening all afternoon, the heavy clouds lending a strange stillness to the city, bringing the old buildings out in eerie relief against the gray sky. Every time I went to glance out one of the back windows in the palazzo today, I would snap away at the sight of the stark figure of Otto Ablenz. The glow of his cigarette, the thought of his cold gaze, that sneer that causes his lips to tilt just so slightly upward has haunted me all afternoon. I cannot leave while he is there. Nico disappeared, off to catch up with old friends, my father told me, watching his grandson go out the front door sadly. He pulled out the newspaper and hid behind it.

At dinnertime, my parents and I sit like three statues at the vast mahogany table in the formal dining room. Papa keeps up a bright conversation with Mama, but his face is pinched, and my mother has been aloof with me since I sat down.

"Nico confessed to me that he is hurt that you are spending time with the New York newspaper man," my mother says, her ringed fingers circling her wine glass. "For your son's sake, give it up, Evelina. You can't travel back in time, and goodness knows, it is a relief that part of your life is over now."

I gasp, stunned, but she continues in a low tone.

"Sometimes middle-aged women like to think that they can behave and look like young girls. This is vanity. You are a mother. You can hardly expect the son of a count to entertain the idea of his mother with some downtown reporter with no ethics. And think about your own reputation. No decent eligible gentleman is going to take someone seriously if they are spending time with a hack."

"Mother! I am not—" I press my lips together. I am not going to lie to her again. The thought is powerful and takes me aback. I look at her, in the comfort of her cardigan, her matching silk blouse, the deep red woolen skirt and the silver brooch pinned to her lapel. When I was nineteen, twenty, I listened to her. I wanted desperately to please her, and I did so the only way I knew how. I married the man she wanted me to marry. I let the love I felt for Jack go cold. It wasn't difficult when he had hurt me so deeply. And yet somewhere, deep inside me, there was always a tiny flicker of hope that one day we might meet again. And now we have.

I miss Arturo of course. Even though our relationship was never simple, because I was broken-hearted over Jack when we met, Arturo showed me that there was a safe place you could go to when things were bad, and for me, it became that beautiful Villa Rosa, which is now my home. He rescued me and captured my heart. But now he is gone.

"Nico needs security. The last thing he needs is his mother cavorting with some New York journalist, when the situation is so grave. And have you heard from Raf?" Her last question holds a note of hysteria.

"Raf is helping the Allies to break the Gustav Line. Mother, you know this. Please stop."

She stares at me.

I feel the muscles in my neck and shoulders cording, a headache pulses above my eyes. Raf, Nico, Jack, Elisabetta, Talia and Mario. And yet, all my mother can complain about is my reputation?

My father intervenes. "The Germans are resisting, holding out in riverbeds, mountain ranges, anywhere they can."

"Please remember you are not a solo entity." She shakes her head at me and leaves the room.

"Evie," my father says helplessly.

But I stand up and place my napkin on the table. I lean down and place a kiss on my father's head.

"Where are you going?" he asks.

"Out," I say.

I run down to where *Mimi* is moored out the front of the palazzo. Otto Ablenz is still lurking in the lane outside the back gate, but he can't see me out front, so I unmoor *Mimi* hurriedly and, without turning back, I steer her to Elisabetta's house, sheets of rain sliding down my waterproof coat like the tears I have not been able to shed since my argument with Nico three years ago, my father's rain hat perched on my head. Lights from other boats glare at me as we travel up the Grand Canal. It is fortunate that the night is still and there is no wind to buffet the water, to skew the trees on the banks into odd shapes, to render the lagoon angry and wild.

Finally, I moor *Mimi* behind Elisabetta's apartment, and run to the front door. When I press the doorbell, Jack appears, silhouetted against the light.

He stands aside for me, and I only send him a brief glance before rushing past him, wanting to find Talia, needing certainty that she is still safe.

. . .

Later, I sit in Talia's bedroom with her. We are both propped up against her pillows, like we used to do when we were young. The thick silk curtains are drawn, and we are on high alert. If anyone comes near the apartment, we will run to the attics, grab Mario, and hide. I cannot bear to tell her that Otto Ablenz is watching me, but this fear curls like a dark ghost around my heart. All it will take is one false move on my part, and Talia will be removed, herded into one of the Nazi cattle trucks and that will be the end.

Talia squeezes my hand, and I turn to her, grateful, suddenly for the fact that we are here together. I must remember that. No matter how little time we might have.

"Tell me what I've missed these last months, Talia," I say. It is such a relief to be here, with my friend who does not judge me harshly.

"Mario's mother, Fedora, was, or... is a great friend of mine," Talia says. "She was writing to her Jewish friends in Germany right through from the mid-thirties, encouraging them to be brave, not to give up their rights. But as the years wore on, and Hitler's policies became increasingly dangerous for us, she began helping Jewish citizens to escape the country. She organized passports and travel arrangements for over twenty families to travel to America, but then it became difficult, and so many countries would not take refugees. And when the Nazis invaded, I was working with her to find safe passage for the children who had been orphaned. Children in my school, in my class. I could not leave them, Nina."

"I wouldn't have thought anything less of you," I say honestly.

"I don't know what I thought was going to happen when I decided to stay in Venice after you did so much for Papa and me," she admits. "I think I was pretending, hoping that what was unfolding in Germany would never touch Italy's shores and that somehow I would be safe. I mean, this is my home!" She turns to me, and I'm glad she can finally unburden herself. "But now, can I confess something?"

I press her cold hand with my own. "Always," I whisper.

"I'm scared."

The nasty little headache above my eyes pulses harder. "I will take care of you," I say.

"You can't fix everything, Nina."

I rest my aching head against the pillows.

"I admired Fedora's bravery, and when I was working alongside her, I felt that I was achieving something, but I don't know..." she says, her voice catching. "Whether I should have left with Papa." She buries her head in her hands for a moment. "I have not heard from him since he left and now I don't know if he made it to America, if he is safe or not. But I couldn't leave," she adds, her shoulders shaking. "I couldn't leave Venice and... the children. Me, selfishly taking a safe passage to America and leaving them here." She turns her head, her face red and blotched with tears. "Do you understand that? Do you understand my dilemma? How impossible it was for me to walk away and leave the children who were in my care, Nina, to their fates?"

I nod, fighting the sense of powerlessness that is starting to overwhelm me. I must focus on helping her. Must focus on helping Mario too. It is all I can do.

"Yes, the Jewish school in our quarter closed down in September, but I was allowed to stay teaching in the state school, when you thought I was on my way to Palestine." She lowers her head again as if trying to stave off a wave of nausea. "I brought several of my Jewish students with me to the Italian state school, including Mario. It was tough for them, but I was able to keep their education going and then, with Fedora's help, I managed to find safe passages for some of them out of Italy. Not all." She shudders violently, and I take her hand. "The remaining children have been rounded up, Nina."

I feel a sense of emptiness, my insides turning numb.

"The work that Fedora and her husband are still doing is dangerous. They are high up on the list of wanted renegades in Venice. Fedora asked me to look after Mario because she felt it was too dangerous for him to be with them and their resistance cell."

I nod. "Of course."

But Talia shakes her head. "Now I have no idea whether Fedora and her husband are alive or dead. They would never have left Mario alone in my house all night if they were alive. Nina..." She pauses, changing tack. "Even in 1938, when the laws changed for Jews, I still held faith in my own country. I never thought Italy would go down the path of Germany, even though Mussolini was shaking hands with Hitler on the front pages of our newspapers. And when Mussolini was stood down last summer, for a brief moment I cheered along with everybody else, hoping that by joining the Allies we had shaken off any risk. Until the Nazis came and made sure of it.

"But after the decree in Verona, I knew things were going to be different. The Italian police who had protected me and allowed me to teach their children at school were completely overridden by the new Nazi laws. A few hours after the conference came the announcement that all Jews were to be deported, and I was told by a neighbor that they would be coming for me that night. Knowing that I could not drag Mario through the streets, I managed to get a message to his parents, asking them to come and collect him. They confirmed they would. I knew I had to run. It was the hardest decision I have ever made in my life." She rubs her arms with her hands. "I left, and now I know that soon afterwards, the Nazis indeed came to our house to take me away. Mario must've heard the whole thing. It is he who is incredibly brave, hiding while they were searching the house."

"But they did not destroy anything in your home."

She turns to me, her huge eyes sad. "No, the nuns told me that the house has been requisitioned for a Nazi."

Otto Ablenz.

I turn to her. "Let me find out where Mario's parents are. I'll find them, reunite him with them, and then I need to get you out of Italy."

She leans back on the pillows, her beautiful eyes closed. "It is not me that I am worried about," she whispers. "It is that innocent little boy."

CHAPTER 19

Talia falls asleep just before midnight, and I let myself out of her room, my thoughts troubled after what she has told me. The chances of us finding Mario's parents will be incredibly slim. And she is right, if they never came for their child after Talia escaped the Nazis, then it does seem likely that they have been transported or killed.

Jack is sitting at his desk in the sitting room, working away on his typewriter. I stand in the doorway a moment, thinking about the huge risk he is taking by sending coded reports back to the United States, reminding myself that his life is at stake too.

I walk over to him, and Elisabetta looks up from where she is reading a book on the sofa.

"I think we should let them sleep for a couple of hours," I say to Jack. "But then I think we should move them. It's too risky leaving them here." I glance across at Jack's grandmother. How could I live with myself if she were taken away too?

I always felt the same sense of home here that I did in Talia's house. These people, Jack, Talia, Elisabetta, and Doctor and Signora Baruch, meant everything to me.

Elisabetta closes the pages of her book and regards me.

Slowly, she removes her reading glasses and places them down on the coffee table in front of her. "Come and sit with me, dear," she says.

I catch Jack's eye and see the twinkle in it.

The invitation to sit with the kindly older woman feels so inviting right now that I can't bear to refuse her, even though I should be making plans with Jack.

"How are you, my dear?" Elisabetta asks.

I sink down into the sofa, and she leans forward and pours me a tiny glass of port wine from a carafe on the coffee table, the glass decorated with imprints of vines and grapes. They remind me of my home in Tuscany.

I accept the glass gratefully. Perhaps a little false courage will not go astray at this time.

"I am well," I say, in answer to her question.

Elisabetta looks at me knowingly. "I would hate to intrude, but if you would like to be my guest too, then you are very welcome." She eyes me. "You know, you are always welcome to stay here."

I can't look at Jack.

The room is silent.

Elisabetta is quiet for a moment, but then she nods to herself, as if she has made up her mind. She looks pointedly at Jack. "Ever since you were young," she says to him, "I have wanted you to meet the right person. But you never did. Your mother always told me that there was someone special in your past, that she thought a boat had sailed away from you, and that you were chasing it constantly, deep in your heart. She told me that she admired you because you were true to yourself and were not going to settle for anyone who was not quite right. That was kind of you, my darling Jack, not to put anyone else in a position where they were not the one you genuinely loved. But it has been a hard road for you. And I am going to be perfectly honest: I believe that person was darling Evelina."

I am staring down at my port wine. I could not be more acutely aware of Jack across the room if I tried.

"Cara Evelina and Jack, who knows how many days we all have left, who knows how this war will end. The only thing I do know is that we must seize life while we have it. And we must not turn down the opportunity to truly love." The elderly lady eases herself up out of her seat and regards us. "Goodnight, brave Evelina," she says. She goes and stands in the doorway. "Take care of your friend and the child. And, my offer stands, my dear. You are welcome to stay with me anytime."

"But I will take Talia and Mario elsewhere," I say to her. "I cannot risk you, Elisabetta." I smile at her, and wish her goodnight, and she slips out the door to her room.

The air is charged in Elisabetta's absence. I take in a shaky breath. Jack frowns at the floor, rolls his sleeves up. He stands up, turns his chair around and sits on it backwards, facing me.

"I think we should move Talia and Mario too." He smiles, and for a moment the dimples in his cheeks dent like they used to when he was young. "If my grandmother is caught, they won't care that she is an elderly woman. These people have no boundaries when it comes to cruelty, Lina. And, you see, the thing about my grandmother is that she has no boundaries when it comes to love." He pauses. "I have spoken to the head waiter at Café Florian. Luciano has agreed to afford Talia and the children safe rooms." His expression is almost unreadable, but his eyes are locked on mine. "I am torn as to whether or not you should go into hiding too. If, as you say, you are on the Nazis' list, they will show no mercy. I cannot..."

I sink back against the cushions.

"I could not, that is I could not live..." Jack leans forward and buries his head in his hands. "I don't know what to do," he says.

"I do," I say softly. "I need to get Talia and Mario out of Venice, but the risks in doing so..." I drag my hands through my hair as if in an attempt to avoid rubbing them together, over and over again. "If we are caught, then I've taken far too much of a risk with them. And I can't afford to act until I have a complete plan in place. And it needs to involve *Mimi*, and must be timed perfectly so that we can pass by the Nazi patrols without getting caught in the lagoon."

He stays quiet.

"I'm not scared of their questions," I whisper. "Not for me. I'm only terrified for Talia and Mario."

"I am," Jack whispers. "For you."

"Jack," I whisper, my voice lingering in the room. "Look at what you are doing, look at what you are risking, your own life. You must realize that I view myself in the same way."

He raises his head, rubs his hand across his chin. There is a paleness around his lips.

"If we give in to fear, then we are letting them win."

"Where will you stay in the meantime?" he asks, his eyes raking over mine. "The palazzo is being watched. You won't be able to go anywhere, do anything, without them knowing. Lina, how did you get on with Nico?"

"Well," I say honestly. "We spoke. I trust him."

Jack's shoulders visibly drop with relief.

"Perhaps I should check into a luxury hotel," I say, my eyes twinkling. "With pink champagne on tap, a view of the sea..."

"And one where, preferably, you can remain in your pajamas all day." He sends me a sad smile.

"And strut up and down the beach like a young fool and enjoy all the attention," I whisper.

"You were wonderful," he murmurs.

"So were you."

For what seems like a long moment, we sit silently, until, finally, he stands up and walks over to me, holding out his hand. Briefly, I hesitate, staring at it, knowing that if I accept it, it will feel like every one of my nerve endings is on fire.

But he stands there, with his hand out, and I can't help it, I take it, and he pulls me to my feet, encircles me in his arms, and after a while, we begin dancing to some silent old tune. My head rests on his shoulder, my body curving into his as naturally as it always did, leaning in toward him, feeling like it's at home.

"We met in a different world, one that we must always hold close, and never let slip away..." he says. He strokes my hair, his fingers soft against the blond tendrils, his touch always was so tender. "This is what we are fighting for, Lina. This."

"I wish I could stay here," I say boldly.

"You can." His voice is rough.

But I shake my head. I reach up and trace a finger around the contour of his cheek.

He leans down and kisses me, his lips brushing mine, and then seeking me out, just as he used to. And in that moment it's as if the war doesn't matter, as if it has been folded away into nothing.

Jack takes in a shaky breath. "I've waited so long to hold you again. I'd given up, but when I heard about Italy, I had to come back. I couldn't not be here."

I pull back, the moment gone, memories flashing through my mind. An emerald ring, a pair of tickets to New York to meet his parents and his brothers, his green eyes alive with hope, the world spread out like a table laid with a banquet before us.

He never fought for me.

And I blamed him, blamed him for the fact that he had just walked away. Sailed away, in fact, back to New York. The thing was, I had given up on my mother years before. But Jack, Jack was supposed to be different. He was supposed to be the one who swept me up and took me away from the cold world where I had been raised. From the world where my mother ran my life as if I was a cog in her wheel, one of her limbs, a stray piece of hair that was slightly wild and out of control and had to be combed back into place.

And when he left, when Jack turned around and went back home to New York, I did not forgive him, nor did I understand. Because I know that if I was him, I would have fought for what we had but I also know now, that I had to find what I hoped to find with him, in myself.

It was not until after Arturo died, not until long after he had died, that I realized I had somehow looked to both these men to rescue me from my childhood. And it has only been since Arturo's tragic death that I have realized that all the strength I needed was inside of me.

And now that I know that? Jack is back. But how can our relationship move forward on a completely different ground?

I look at him, a foot's width between us. "I shall take them to the Café Florian very early before Venice wakes," I whisper.

The look in his eyes is impossible to read. "And I will guard you like the most loyal vigilante, all the way," he says.

"And I you," I whisper back.

A frisson of something dark whispers, featherlike, through my insides.

I wake to the sound of Elisabetta moving about in the kitchen, to the smell of brewing coffee, and the feel of Jack's arms encircling me on the sofa. I have enjoyed several hours of unbroken sleep for the first time since I arrived in Venice, albeit fully dressed with my shoes still on.

Jack leans down and places a kiss on the top of my head. "Good morning, darling," he murmurs. I turn around, propping myself up on my elbow.

It is pitch dark outside. No cracks of light permeate the edges of the blackout curtains.

But Elisabetta, laden with a tray bearing espressos, bread and preserves and sliced oranges, comes into the room and sets the breakfast down on the coffee table. "I thought you could do with some sustenance. I set my alarm," she says firmly.

My lips curve in a smile, and Jack sits up, thanking his grandmother, spreading conserves on the bread, the ripe fresh oranges reminding me of hope, and the sun.

"Venice is full of secret passages and hiding places," Elisabetta reminds me. "Use them on the way to Café Florian, both of you."

I nod and take a sip of the strong coffee. It wakes me up and I feel the customary fear and excitement that has been my companion since I came back to the city of my youth. The thing about being isolated in a lagoon on a set of islands is there is no uncomplicated way to escape. You need to hide within.

Perhaps that is where the Nazis have underestimated Venice. Our buildings may be standing on wooden foundations, but they—and we—are strong. This sense of solidarity with the city I love, and the people I love, two of whom are in this room, strengthens me, and I down my coffee and break some bread.

Jack and I help Elisabetta clean up after we have eaten, and she chatters away as if to pass the time, but occasionally her voice flutters, and she sends a worried look Jack's way.

In the bathroom, I wash quickly, splash my face with water, rinse out my mouth. When I step back out into the hallway, Elisabetta is knocking on Talia's door, a shot of coffee, bread and preserves ready for her. Jack is waking the sleeping little boy.

Where his parents are, I cannot imagine, but I understand that Talia wants to find them, if we can, before we leave for Tuscany.

Mario seems achingly aware when our little party gathers in Elisabetta's living room. He stands with Talia, holding her hand.

"Now," Talia says, "you must not talk, all the way to our new hiding place. You understand?"

He looks up at his teacher solemnly, and nods.

I take in a shaky breath. Jack and I share a long glance, and I feel a fleeting sense of dread that I may not see him again but there's no time to dwell on this.

It is time to enact our plan.

I am to take Mario first. My body wrapped in a warm coat, boots zipped up firmly, I lean down and sweep the child up into my arms. It will be a slight strain carrying him the entire way, but I do not want to risk us not being able to move quickly if we hear footsteps.

Jack pulls us both into a hug, then I am enfolded in Talia's arms for a brief moment. Before Mario and I disappear out into the quiet morning.

I have borrowed a pair of Elisabetta's rubber-soled boots. They are silent as possible on the cobblestones, and Mario buries his head in my shoulder.

When I finally step out into St. Mark's Square, my eyes dart about like a criminal. It was all very well to take the back lanes, to hide in the silent shadows, but there is no getting around the fact that I need to either cross the square or creep around its edges to get to the famous Café Florian.

The square is silent, deadly dark and cold. Only a few loose pieces of paper, shifting about in the sharp breeze, give any sign of movement here. I make my way around the edge of the famous piazza, my eyes darting everywhere, on high alert. When I come to the closed door of Café Florian, I knock quietly, and the head waiter, kindly Luciano, lets me in.

I stretch my back, and I glance outside as Luciano holds the door open for a second. And in that moment, I feel the definite sensation that someone is watching me. That I have been followed. I tell myself that it is only my sense of dread for Talia and Jack, who will be coming shortly.

I crouch down and speak to Mario. "You can trust Signor Luciano," I say to him, taking his face in my hands, gently stroking a stray eyelash from his cheek.

The little boy, who has been through so much through no fault of his own, nods and places his hand in Luciano's.

The waiter, his gray hair thinning on his head, and his chin marked with early-morning stubble, speaks to the little boy. "I am going to take you upstairs now, and we shall wait for your teacher," he says. "I have put some books and puzzles up in the attics. They belonged to my children when they were your age. Would you like that?"

Mario nods. Solemnly. My heart goes out to him, and the way he is so grateful for having a roof over his head.

"I shall expect my next guest in twenty minutes," he says to me.

I nod. We have timed things so that we won't cross paths.

I slip back out into the darkness, the turrets and domes of the San Marco Cathedral sitting still in the shadows. I wrap my arms around my body as if to make myself smaller, tuck my head down, and make my way around the edge of the square.

But as I slip through the shadows, a man steps out in front of me, blocking my way. Even in the inky darkness, I can read the expression on his face. I can see the too close-blue eyes, the knowing smile as his lips curve into a crooked smile, the cold, hardness underneath.

I shudder, and he grabs my arm and drags me across the piazza while the shadowy turrets and domes of San Marco watch over me.

I don't even have time to scream.

CHAPTER 20

The air seems to close in on me. I am dragged across the square by Otto Ablenz, and before I know what is happening, a door opens into one of the gorgeous old buildings that line the square in my home city, and I'm in a room where a bare lightbulb swings from the ceiling. A bath of water sits in the corner. Ice cubes float in it. And behind a desk, surrounded by cigar smoke, sits Wilhelm Moritz, the Nazi commander of Venice, eyeing me over the tops of his half-moon glasses.

I am slammed down into a cold hard chair.

Moritz sits back, stretches his arms, wafting smoke through the already stench-filled air. He places the cigar down in an ashtray, cracks his wrists, and then each finger, one by one.

"Well, well," he says. "What have we here?"

My heart sinks. How much have they seen? Did they see me carrying Mario to the Café Florian? Is our cover blown? I close my eyes. Talia and Jack will be outside any moment. Perhaps I can keep these awful men here as a distraction. Perhaps it will afford the others some time.

"You have been hiding a Jew."

I sit up tall, press my lips closed.

Wilhelm sends a glance toward the cold bath in the corner. Horribly, he reaches out, and takes my hands in his own. His fingers are icy cold, and I notice that his fingernails are filthy. Dirty. When he smiles, his teeth are yellow. Up close, the stink of cigar smoke is unbearable. "There's no point in arguing. We know everything."

I tip my head back and eye him, but remain tight-lipped.

"Let me make it easy for you," he says, leering across the desk toward me. "You are a beautiful, intelligent woman, and I'm sure you'll understand me."

My lip curls.

"We are seeking two dissidents, Fedora and Lino Di Maggio, who are deliberately setting out to disrupt the Third Reich. They are enemies, traitors of the regime, whom we have long needed to curb. They set out to create problems, signora. I believe you have their child."

I remain silent.

He tightens his grip on my fingers, pressing his fleshy hands so hard into mine that the bones in my fingers feel like they will crack.

"It depends upon how you play this, signora."

I try to concentrate on my breathing. But Moritz flicks a glance toward the door, and Otto, towers in behind me, fencing me in.

"These Jews have caused great trouble," Moritz whispers. He exerts a sharp squeeze on my hands again. I do not flinch.

He kicks my shin under the table, sending a sharp twang all the way up my leg, but I do not budge.

He narrows his eyes. "Very well, Contessa. As long as you have their child, we know that the parents will eventually find their way to him. We shall keep watching and waiting. We have time."

My stomach sickens.

"Or you can tell me where the parents are hiding, and

perhaps we won't have to kill the child along with his parents, whose crimes are punishable by death. Do you understand me, or not?"

The Nazis don't know I have Talia.

And then, something else. In my heightened state, I had not allowed myself to feel a sense of relief that Mario's parents have not been transported.

"So," Wilhelm Moritz eyes the bath, ice pooling around the surface like fish, "what is it going to be, signora?"

I lift my chin.

How could this man possibly not know?

They keep me sitting on a hard wooden seat, the lightbulb hanging from the ceiling shining into my eyes, while they smoke and play card games, and drink Venice's most expensive wines. Every time they get out a new bottle, I want to sneer. My mother always said that pride comes before a fall.

I sit up straight, my head held high, but I remain silent no matter what they say. Their words filter over and around me, their harsh tones never getting near my heart.

As dawn breaks over Venice, Otto Ablenz slips out. Wilhelm Moritz watches him leave, a smile spreading across his features as if he were watching his own child.

I sit and sit and do not talk. Wilhelm barks questions at me, but I don't budge.

Later, Otto returns. He shoves another man into the room. I am at the point I don't care. I am nearly falling off my seat from exhaustion, but then, Jack stumbles across the floor.

They have Jack. My sore hands start shaking, and I try to calm myself with a deep breath.

Otto slams the door to this odious room behind himself.

Jack glances at me, reaches out a hand, but I keep staring

straight ahead, not wanting to catch sight of the smugness in Otto Ablenz's eyes.

Otto pushes a chair across the room roughly, and orders Jack to sit.

I do not turn to look at him. I cannot bear it. Instead, I reach out, and brush his hand with mine.

Otto sees this and yanks my chair a good few feet away from Jack's. I have to cling onto the chair to keep it upright. It feels as if evil has taken reign. Now that Jack is here, this distorted, strange situation feels even more real.

Wilhelm lights another cigar and regards us through the smoke. "It is difficult for me to understand your foolishness. Why you would take such risks."

"And it is difficult for me to see why you would risk the life of a reporter who is sending news back to the United States." Jack speaks coolly, but there is a glint of annoyance in Wilhelm's eyes. "You asked me to tell a favorable story. How am I supposed to do that?"

My stomach stirs darkly.

"I take your treatment of the Contessa very seriously." Jack leans forward in his chair.

Wilhelm taps his cigar in the ashtray. Otto smirks behind him. And then Wilhelm flicks a nod at Otto, who pulls out a gun, and points it at Jack.

"Tell us where your friends are. Now." Wilhelm's cold gaze is terrifying.

I take in a sharp breath.

"I am a news man, not a businessman," Jack says evenly. But his eyes are trained straight on Otto and his gun, and I sense that if Otto moves, Jack will jump up and attempt to restrain him. "I don't do deals. I report the truth. And if you want my head on your plate, there will be an international uproar. I cannot vouch for what my country might do. You are on a losing streak, Moritz. The Allies are on their way. Be careful."

Moritz glares at Jack.

Otto moves closer to him and sticks the gun against his throat.

"Let me make one thing clear," I say suddenly. "I have never met, and do not know the Di Maggios. I have no knowledge as to where they are, and you keeping me here is a waste of your time. We are all busy. As you well know, I have a business to run, and Jack's business is to report back to New York. You can keep us here as long as you wish, but the outcome will remain the same. We know nothing. Neither of us have knowledge of nor have we met these people."

Wilhelm's lip curls.

"I would suggest you let us go," I say, my voice still intoning clear as a bell. "There is no benefit in keeping us any longer."

"If the Di Maggios come anywhere near you, or their son, you will all get the death penalty. It is well deserved." Wilhelm places his cigar down and presses his hands into his desk. "Very well deserved." He rolls his tongue over the words as if he is a connoisseur and death is his drink of choice.

I shudder, and Jack shifts in his seat next to me.

"We are watching you," Wilhelm Moritz says. "At this point, I would rather watch than kill. For now. You will lead us where we need to go. But I may change my mind."

Otto shoves the gun at us, indicating for us to move.

"The Di Maggios will come to you," Wilhelm says. "They will eventually seek their child."

Jack turns just as we are about to exit the room, but I take his hand, my own fingers still sore from the way Wilhelm pressed them with his dirty, meaty paws.

The sun is shining over the Piazza San Marco when we are pushed out of the interrogation rooms. People are out strolling, even if they are looking over their shoulders, huddled and subdued. The tables are set outside the Café Florian. I risk a glance at the windows above the café. Somewhere up there are Talia and that darling little boy.

I glance around the square. When I was a child, I used to look with interest and a disturbing sense of trepidation at the Bridge of Sighs, where prisoners caught their last glimpse of Venice before being taken to the cells that lurk in the dark shadows beneath the Doge's Palace. I have seen them. They are terrifying.

Venice is well set up for the Nazis. The only thing we can be thankful for is the fact that they did not occupy our city in 1940, as they did Paris. I suspect things would have been completely different had they arrived before we all knew the Allies were trying to advance through southern Italy.

Jack pulls me into a quick hug, in full view of everyone in the square. "Lina."

"I am perfectly fine. They did not hurt me."

I clasp Jack's hand and pull him out of the Piazza San Marco. When we are in one of the laneways, I stop.

"Are they safe?" I whisper.

A myriad of expressions passes across his face. He frowns and rubs his chin and looks down at the ground. "Yes," he says finally. "But Otto Ablenz knows Mario is in Café Florian. He told me he saw you."

I close my eyes.

"They grilled me before we came to you, not only about Mario's parents, but about Talia's whereabouts. They think she is at large. They know she was your friend, but they are far more interested in Fedora and Lino Di Maggio. For now."

A chill runs up and down my spine. "But how—"

"They were busy interrogating you when Talia and I crossed the square separately. If they had not caught you, they would have caught her. You saved her, Lina. But I never want to feel as terrified as I did then." His expression darkens.

We start moving again, the rhythm of our footsteps beating alongside the pounding thoughts in my mind. "So where did they intercept you?"

"They didn't. They came to Elisabetta's house after Talia, and I had completed the move. They had you, they wanted me."

I shudder. "Elisabetta?"

"Was formidable. Closed the door in their face. They tried to kick it down, and I went with them. I left her at home."

I slip my hand into his. "I can't bear anything to happen to her."

"It won't," he says.

But fear curls through me. "Was there any mention of the murder of the Nazi?"

Jack shakes his head.

"So, we don't know whether they have made that connection yet."

"They are hardly going to give it away." His voice is gruff, and there is a tiredness in it that I have not heard before.

"Jack, you don't have to remain involved in this. You are already taking such risks..." I don't admit it, but I feel the same way he does. If anything were to happen to him, it would be far worse than something happening to myself.

He turns to me and pulls me into a hug, kisses the top of my forehead so tenderly that I close my eyes. "Does this make things clear?" he murmurs. "If you are in this, I am in this. Always."

I pull back and search his face. I see the dark shadows beneath his eyes. Everyone walks around with a face blanched with fatigue.

A lump forms in my throat, and I wipe my eyes in a bid to stop the tears that are forming behind them. "I don't know how much longer the world can keep going like this, Jack. We need to get them both out of Italy," I say. "The Nazis may be playing a game with us, waiting to see if Mario's parents turn up to claim him, but once they discover he is with Talia, things will be quite different, not only for them, but for my parents, for Elisabetta."

Jack sighs. "I know. They'll only follow you to Tuscany if you take Talia and Mario there, Lina."

I know he's right and begin to accept the truth of it as we come to the back gate of the palazzo. Italy is simply no longer safe. Instinctively, we have both been walking to my parents' house. I think there is an unspoken agreement that we do not want to put Elisabetta at any further risk. She has already done so much.

I place my hand on the gate. I would rather incur Nico's wrath than risk Elisabetta, but walking into my childhood home feels like I'm walking into uncertainty, not safety. If Nico sees me with Jack, how will he react?

As we move through the garden, the sun highlighting the bare, skeletal trees, the flowerbeds sitting fallow and colorless, all I can think is that a long frigid winter is on its way, and for a sudden moment, I miss Tuscany, miss my life there, and the Villa Rosa which is always, no matter what the weather, facing the sun.

My hands are trembling as I open the door to my parents' house. All I want to do is see my son. As I move through the house, I am fixated with this, even though Jack is behind me, following on. I am looking for Nico, desperately telling myself that all is well, my heartbeat quickening as I move through the entrance hall.

Papa comes down the staircase. His eyes dart to me, and their expression is full of such concern that I gasp. He only pauses for one moment, and then he is at the bottom of the stairs and has me in his arms.

"I went for coffee this morning," he says. He holds me tight, like he used to when I was little girl. "Luciano told me that you had been questioned." He lets out a sob. "I had no idea what to think."

I close my eyes. "I am all right," I say. "I am not hurt."

Papa leads us into his sitting room. "I have not said anything to your mother or Nico," he says, closing the door. He turns to Jack, takes his hand, and grips it with both of his. "You were interrogated too?" he asks.

"Don't worry about that. It is Evelina that I was concerned for," Jack says.

Papa nods at Jack with something that looks like respect. Relief washes over me. I know my father viewed Jack's walking away from me in the same way my mother did, as proof that he did not have what it took to be with me.

I sit down, weariness suddenly kicking in as I lean back on Papa's velvet sofa. I close my eyes a moment. Papa asks our elderly housekeeper to prepare coffee and sandwiches.

"It's time you told me the whole story," Papa says.

We are both quiet, but he eyes us.

"The resistance is increasing in Milano," Papa says quietly. "There are reports coming out that those in the resistance cells have been setting off explosives. No deaths. But there is also no news of Nazi reprisals. As yet."

My hands burn where Wilhelm Moritz pressed them so hard.

Papa regards me. "I have looked into Fedora and Lino Di Maggio."

I start.

"I know they are Mario's parents, Evie. How could you think that I'd not discover more about the boy you brought into my home?"

I stay quiet.

"But I don't know whether they are alive, Evie," he says finally. "I'm sorry. Sorry for the child."

I stand up, my hands playing with my necklace now. "I

need to find out if Mario's parents are alive before I take him and Talia out of Venice. I can't take him if they are still here, and separate him from them," I add helplessly.

I rub my hands around and around, only to see Jack's eyes trained on them. I have to force myself to stop.

"I need to know where the Di Maggios are or were operating before they disappeared," I tell my father. "Can you help me with that?"

My father frowns and sits back in his chair.

"Please," I snap, unnecessarily.

"As long as you promise me you won't go looking for them, Evie."

CHAPTER 21

The following morning, I have just finished my breakfast when Nico appears, yawning and stretching in the door to the breakfast room. He stops when he sees me, and then moves toward me, half starting to say something, and then seeming to think the better of it.

"Are you all right, Nico?" I ask him.

He frowns and makes his way into the room, sits down and stares at the fruit and bread as if there is something wrong with it. "Nonna tells me that you have been spending time with the New York journalist." He grimaces at the table.

"Nico..."

He jerks his head up, his eyes ablaze with anger that used to worry me when he was in his teenage years. It is as if I am dealing with that troubled younger version of himself. "What are you planning to do? Go live with him in New York after the war?"

I reach my hand out across the table, but Nico pulls away.

"It is impractical. Have you even thought about the future?"

I stand up, an unsettled feeling simmering through me, and

I move toward the window, take a few deep breaths, and look down at the Grand Canal.

"He is not going to remain in Italy with you. What are you expecting him to do? Settle down and live in Villa Rosa? While you run everything? Nonna and I think you are being naïve."

I tut out loud. Of course, my mother has involved my son in this. I shake my head and sigh.

"A man like that will never settle down. Nonna says he has spent his entire career caravanning around Europe like a gypsy."

I press my lips together, unable to stomach his disparaging reference to gypsies when they have been lumped together with all of Hitler's other undesirables.

"Remember, if you marry him, the Villa Rosa will become his property."

"You are talking of things that are not planned, that I do not envisage happening." Although, deep down, a little part of me had imagined Jack at the Villa Rosa with me.

"I would hate to see you left with nothing, when you marry him, and he has the right to everything we own." His tone is sarcastic.

"I'm hardly speaking of marriage."

"So, you are going to live in sin with him? Is that it? Nonna says you did not come home the other night."

An innocent night slept in our clothes, waiting to help Talia and Mario to safety!

I grip the windowsill and focus on the Santa Maria della Salute church. Her perfect domes sit gray and impermeable against the blue sky.

Nico taps his spoon on the table. "You are a contessa, and you are my mother. People are talking."

I had never thought of my son and my mother being cut from the same cloth.

I gather myself and turn around to face him.

He looks at me expectantly, and a poignancy shoots through me at the hope that is in his eyes.

I force myself to remain calm. "Jack and I knew each other when we were young. We have met up again under extremely unusual circumstances. I don't know what happens after the war. Can you trust me, will you let me work this out?"

Nico's lip curls. "Do you love him?"

His question takes me aback. We are a formal family. Love is not something we speak of openly.

I hold his gaze, but I remain silent, and he pushes his chair back.

"Nico—"

"No, Mama. You have never asked for my opinion on this. What I think, how I feel about it. You simply carry on with no reference toward me. You run Papa's business interests. Have you ever thought that I should be running them? Now, you take up with some American journalist, and then what? Bring him to the Villa Rosa and let him take over what is rightfully mine?"

He moves across to stand beside the fireplace.

I sigh, heavily, and, my heart breaks, because I don't know if I can get through to him and I thought we had made such a breakthrough about Talia.

I clutch at straws. "And you, Nico?" I whisper. "Have you ever fallen in love?"

He barks out a laugh. "Somebody needs to be responsible and take on the business side of things for the family. What I am doing, Mama, is trying to realize profits for us all, so that after the war, when everything falls apart, someone can fund the mess. We have lost a generation of farmers. How are their families going to survive? They will need support, and I am storing up the funds to help them. Do you honestly think that the system under which the tenant farmers who have put up with our family's ownership of the farms since the thirteen hundreds is going to hold up after this showdown?" He folds his arms.

"There will be nothing left once the Allies have been through, crops destroyed, farms blown up."

"I know," I say. We have won no battles, followed a madman, and we are paying for it now. We are already struggling to feed our people."

"There is talk of a mass exodus to the New World—New York, Australia, those places that have not been devastated by war. My generation are going to want a better start in life than Italy can offer them. Are you going to abandon Italy too? Go to New York with your lover?"

"He is not my lover..." I refuse to discuss such matters with my son.

But a muscle in Nico's cheek tweaks. "It is going to be extremely difficult for you to carry on as you were before the war. Mother, you must accept that the world is going to change. I have also heard that landowners are going to have to *give* property they own to their tenant farmers to try to get them to stay. It is too much for you to deal with alone. We are a family. The American has no place with us."

I curl my fingers into fists, digging my fingernails into my palms, but my hands ache terribly from the pain that Wilhelm Moritz inflicted on them yesterday. Nico does not know that I was taken in for questioning. My mother does not know. They focus on Jack. Jack, who is trying to help where I suspect my son would refuse to help. If my mother is manipulating my son to try to turn me against Jack, then I must be wary. This is a complication that Talia, and those children do not need.

"You must rely on my good sense," I say to my son, but he presses on.

"Manufacturing, new inventions, this is going to be the way forward after the war. Getting people back to work. Once the ammunition business dies down, we need to start working with innovators, and Italy is famous for its wonderful-quality goods. I want to buy one of the factories in Milano, and start a business making superior leather goods. I will send back funds to support our interests in Tuscany, so that we don't have to sell off all the family property, so that you can support the widows and children who will be left with no skills to farm. The elderly. So, they don't all leave."

I press my fingers into my eyebrows. He is still my son, he still wants the right things.

But I must work out a way to get Mario to safety. Ideally, we need to find his parents. We need to reunite this family.

All I want in my heart is a proper relationship with my eldest child. I feel awful. Like any mother, I want to have the time for my son. But the situation with that other little boy is pressing.

"You need to end whatever this infatuation is with the New Yorker. It will not end well. You and I need to work together to ensure the best outcome for our tenants, for our family. And you must stop putting my grandparents at risk. What were you thinking? Bringing a Jewish boy we don't know into our home?"

I almost stagger backwards in shock. My eyes graze against my own son's steely expression.

"I am sorry you feel this way," I say simply.

Nico lowers his voice, glances out at the century-old hallway. The only sound is a ticking clock softly resonating into the room. "Let me run the business side of things. You only need an apartment, and you could move to Milano. It is the center of culture and taste. The Villa Rosa is too big for a woman. You shouldn't be living there alone. When I marry, I will move my family into it."

Give up the Villa Rosa? And give up Jack?

"You are going to be unable to manage it."

I turn back to face the church of Santa Maria della Salute. I grew up thinking that our lives were determined by fate. When I was young, I thought that fate had led me to fall in love with Jack. But I am a woman, and that is how we were raised, before we were thrust into this war. My mother taught me that love came with marriage, stability, family, duty.

I stand here and look out at a church that was built in thanks for the divine intervention of fate, God and the Virgin Mary to bring about the end of tragedy in our city, and yet part of me knows that Nico is right. I cannot see Jack settling down in the Villa Rosa, and I could not bear to leave Italy and travel to America to be with him. Being his secretary adjunct, following him around if he wishes to continue working as an international reporter, is not something I could do. I have become too used to living my own life. I don't want to give that up.

I wipe a stray tear from my cheek. I must acknowledge that I have come to treasure my independence since Arturo died.

I turn to my son. I need to make one thing clear. I cannot have Nico running my life, just as I know I could not have Jack running it.

But my son stares at me defiantly. Sometimes your family can push you in ways no one else can. War feels like it is encircling me in a spiral that rings out from my own heart to my family, to my country and beyond.

"I have not thought beyond the war when it comes to Jack, but I will not have you telling me how to live my life, Nico. No more of this. No more."

He turns around and presses his hands into the fireplace, lowering his head and staring at the floor. All I can see is tension in his broad shoulders, the corded muscles. "And I thought love was about family." He turns and faces me, his expression raw. "All I am trying to do is protect you. Because my father is no longer here."

"Nico..." Heat tingles on my cheeks. I thought I had reached him, but his stubborn arrogance is still there.

He glares at me, and he turns around and walks out of the room.

CHAPTER 22

Nico leaves for Milano an hour after our conversation. As we stand in the grand entrance hall, with the front door thrown wide open, and the water taxi waiting with its engine purring outside on the landing place, Nico hugs my mother.

"*Arrivederci*, Nonna," he says to her, holding her close.

She regards me over his shoulder. "I am always here for you, Nico," she murmurs. "No matter what, my darling. You can count on me, you know that."

I wince at the veiled meaning in those words.

My father kisses him on both cheeks, then holds him close a moment and says something indistinguishable.

Finally, my son turns to me. "I don't like your boyfriend," Nico murmurs. "I trust that next time I see you, the American will be gone."

My father murmurs something low and sympathetic next to me, but even as I watch my eldest son departing, even as my heart breaks for the way we cannot connect, for the fact that I feel torn, I know if I give into him, I shall be untrue to myself, and if I am not true to myself, how is that a way to live?

. . .

That afternoon, my father calls me into his sitting room. I take in the lines across his forehead, the worried expression in his eyes.

"It turns out that Fedora and Lino Di Maggio are—or were —with the Garibaldi-Fruili division of so-called communists in Venice, who are liaising with other communist groups throughout Italy, and collectively, that group are planning to scale up their attacks in coming months. Fedora and Lino are— or were—two of the rebel leaders among Venice's communist groups. It is unclear whether they are alive or have been imprisoned. I could not establish an answer for you. I'm sorry, Evie."

"Oh, poor Mario." I shake my head. I want answers for him, and I hate to take him away, not knowing whether or not his parents are alive. What would I tell him? How would I answer his inevitable questions once we are in Tuscany? No, I need to find out, and I am the only person who can do so. The child deserves to know more than nothing. And that is what he knows now.

My father leans forward in his seat and clasps his hands between his knees. "Mario's parents were living in Castello, not far from the arsenal, with their particular group."

"And you have an address in Castello?"

"I do."

It is known as the most authentic part of Venice, ancient, modest stone houses, laneways with washing hanging overhead. In Castello, generations of simple Venetian folk have lived out their lives. I am not surprised that those who are fighting against powerful fascist rulers are wanting to hide away in an area that might remind them of different times. And even in Tuscany I have heard talk that the partisans prefer to seek out help in the poorer areas of Italy, because they feel that they will be more kindly received. That is fair enough. For two decades,

Mussolini has been the preferred leader of the rich.

"You must not go there. Definitely not." The golden clock ticks on Papa's mantelpiece. "An elderly couple were allowing the partisans to live with them."

Even more risky then. I am silent, and I glance at my papa.

"Are you all right, Evie?" he asks.

"Of course," I nod. As much as I want to get Mario to his parents, I cannot risk drawing attention to the family who are affording him shelter. It seems that every act of daring and courage that we carry out to try to help one innocent citizen living under the Nazi regime comes at significant risk to another.

Perhaps it was simply too dangerous for Mario's parents to come and collect him from Talia's house. What if something went wrong with the message from Talia to come and collect their son? What if they are still waiting for Talia, and they are not aware she is in hiding, and that their son is safe? No, both son and parents deserve to know where the other is.

I straighten my woolen skirt. "I shall go there during the festival of Santa Maria della Salute. I cannot bear to take him away from Venice without trying to do all I can to find his parents," I add, my voice wavering, understanding what it is to be a mother while not knowing whether your child is safe.

"I worry it is too dangerous." Papa's tone is full of concern. "It is too far for you to go from San Marco to Castello. And I hate to tell you this, but tomorrow they are forecasting an *acqua alta*. Floods."

"Santa Maria," I murmur. If the forecast is correct, many of the canals will burst their banks, and seep excess water into the city. "Have you the sandbags ready?" I ask my father.

"Of course. But that is not what I am worried about."

"I shall walk to Café Florian at ten o'clock, and find out all I can from Talia. Tell her my plan."

My father eyes me.

But I hold his gaze. I shall move forward and find out what has happened to Mario's parents before I take him away from them, come rain, come shine.

Later, I am in my mother's bedroom. Tomorrow is the festival of Maria della Salute. The festival tradition dictates that we cross a makeshift bridge made of pontoons that support a walkway across the Grand Canal to the church. We light candles at the altar, in thanks for the Virgin Mary's bringing the terrifying plague of Venice to an end five hundred years ago, and outside in the church square, there is a market, then, everyone goes home for a special dinner.

I used to sit in here when I was young, watching my mother get dressed to go to the opera, balls, the Carnevale. I remember she used to have the most elaborate, exquisite masks imaginable for the festival that encapsulates the spirit of Venice every February. I would sit while she touched up her lipstick, dabbed rouge on her smooth cheeks, brushed eyeshadow across the lids of her wide brown eyes.

Now, I go to her largest armoire. I pull open one of the doors, revealing the collection of wigs for the Carnevale, each kept in shape by being stored atop a head fashioned out of soft wood. There are Marie Antoinette confections, 1920s shingled bob, elegant nineteenth-century updos.

I reach for a light brown, inconspicuous one, shingled, and lift it from its wooden dome. Carefully, I wrap it in a calico traveling bag and place it in a carrier bag that I have brought with me. As I turn to leave, I glance toward the window and grimace at the thought of Otto Ablenz watching, but I don't for a moment mean to make any changes to my plan.

"You are a fool if you think that man is going to be as easy to manage as your late husband."

I take in a breath, but when I turn to see my mother

standing in the doorway, it feels as if a spiderweb is wrapping around my chest. "I was never trying to manage Arturo."

My mother reaches for her packet of cigarettes, lights one, and blows out a perfect smoke ring, eyeing my bulging carrier bag. "We are more alike than you realize, you and me. And Nico."

I press my lips together.

"I chose well for you," she says. "Arturo was the right man for you, Evelina."

I regard the woman whom I have tried and failed to please all my life. When I was young, I rebelled, but, at heart, I think I was trying to get her attention all the time. *Look at me, look at me*, I was shouting inwardly when I went to the Lido. *I can be daring, and sophisticated, and, well, darned strong too.*

And now, she tells me that I am like her. But I realize, with sudden, brimming clarity, that I do not have to be like her to be part of this family. Yes, I am an excellent businesswoman and I've run Arturo's interests as well as any man, but I also want to be a person who helps. A person who cares, who has compassion. Because, goodness knows, it is what the world needs. We have an entire nation trained out of it marching around the world.

So, despite my efforts to try to gain her acceptance, I realize that in doing so, I have only resolutely become myself. "Arturo and I complemented each other, because we each had different skills," I tell my mother. "Our marriage worked because we let each other be who we were."

My mother smiles and comes to slide down on one of the velvet chairs in her dressing room. "I have always wanted you to be who you are. You don't appreciate that. I knew you would be happy with Arturo because he would let you be yourself; he would not constrict you. You must understand I wanted what was best for you." She taps her cigarette on the ashtray. "Do you think you can be yourself with the journalist?"

"He has a name. And it is Jack."

"I know."

I clutch the wig, hopelessly trying to count the seconds until I can leave.

"He will expect you to follow what he does. He's nothing like Arturo. Be careful."

I hold her gaze, my eyes locked with hers. My mother has a catlike beauty that can come across as confronting, but now I see its strength, her intelligent understanding, perhaps, of me. Does she know me better than I thought she did?

I know, deep down, about Jack. He has his life. I have mine. How is that supposed to work in the long term when my life is so firmly based at the Villa Rosa and his is centered not around a home but around traveling Europe to tell stories and sell them back to America? At the end of this war, it is very clear that people will want to know what's happened, and those journalists who can access the truth... the horrors, are going to be vital in spreading the stories that I can only pray will stop another world war from ever happening again.

Nico said it, my mother is saying it. Jack will not want to settle down in one place. After all, he walked out last time as quickly as he could when my mother challenged him.

I sigh heavily. "Look, I don't know what happens after the war ends. All I want to do is get Talia and Mario to safety right now. Jack and I, we..." I shrug.

"Don't give up the freedom that you have at the Villa Rosa," my mother whispers. "Arturo gave you freedom, Evelina, a title, a home, and a position as a woman that will give you great reward. I hope, one day, you will understand that that is what I wanted for you."

I look at her, struggling to find the right words. I wonder if she knows about Nico's plan for me: a small flat in Milano. I feel a light-headedness that I have never experienced before when it comes to my mother. I have always thought of her as a person who was constricting me. Now, I am unsure.

CHAPTER 23

The following morning, I wake early. It is the sound of beating rain against my bedroom window that stirs me. I pull aside the blackout curtains, and the rain is falling like glass beads onto the water below my window, and the sounds of Papa and our housekeeper hauling sandbags filters up through the old house.

I pull on my dressing gown quickly, hating the fact that they are working so early without me, and I rush downstairs. The *acqua alta* is a Venetian fact of life between October and March, but it is one that we can do without today. I try not to panic about the fact that I need to get to Castello through this weather, even if I have a disguise.

The front door to the palazzo is open, and not caring that I am in my dressing gown, I help Papa and our elderly house-keeper move the sandbags that they have brought up from the cellars to provide a barrier between our landing stage and the front entrance. I glance across at our neighbor's house. Their front entrance is fully protected. Despite the deluge, and the fact that San Marco Square will most probably be decorated with makeshift walkways on stilts today, I know it will not be long before the workers begin setting up the pontoons and the temporary bridge across the Grand Canal to the church of Santa Maria della Salute for today's festival. Nothing will stop Venice from commemorating this important event.

Once we have taken care of the entrance to the palazzo, Papa and I, soaking wet in the pouring rain, and the house-keeper with her gray hair dripping, move inside, and place a barrage of sandbags against the interior of the front door.

It is heavy work, and it has woken me up completely, while providing a good distraction from the trepidation I feel about today's task. Finally, I close the great front door to the palazzo as the first pink streaks of dawn appear in the sky.

After I have had breakfast and fielded questions from my mother as to what I am doing today, I allow precisely enough time to get to San Marco, to go up to the top floor of the Café Florian and to tell Talia what I am doing, and then to make my way to Castello. Despite the rain falling about my ankles and getting into my boots, I feel a frisson of excitement that my patient little friend might get to see his parents again if this all works out.

But Otto Ablenz is waiting for me under a black umbrella outside the back gate.

I quicken my pace once I am past him. He walks slightly behind me, but I soon gain on him, because I am used to walking in Venetian rain.

But still, the memories of that bare lightbulb, of the knowing sneer on Willhelm Moritz's face, haunt me as I move toward my destination.

I come to the Piazza San Marco, knowing that I can lose him here, as it is teeming with people. Umbrellas are up, and the crowds are moving slowly. Fearful eyes dart around anxiously, and people talk in soft murmurs as I make my way through their perfect protective screen. Over near the cathedral, men are starting to put up the wooden walkways that we use for the *acqua alta*, but for the moment, the Venetians are sloshing about in the rain.

I duck and weave past people's umbrellas, out of the square here, into a laneway there, only to emerge back again closer to the Café Florian every time. But despite my small triumph—I seem to have lost him—I feel an uneasiness settling over me because my fellow citizens seem to be so quiet. There is not the usual camaraderie in the streets, families walking together, the elderly stopping to pat each other on the back, to discuss the feast they will be enjoying after their pilgrimage to the church of Sanat Maria della Salute. We have our festival, but it is subdued.

I come to Café Florian, and the doorman lets me in without question. I go in as the Contessa Messina, but I shall leave as someone else.

The chandeliers are ablaze, Nazis in uniform are seated in the famous banquettes under the frescoes that always make the famous café feel like an eighteenth-century salon. I turn my nose up in the air as I pass a Nazi with his arm around a girl.

Even though it gives me immense pleasure to reassure myself that Otto Ablenz has lost me, I suspect he has not. But I worry about the web of connections in here since I have walked in among all these Nazis.

My hands tremble as I make my way through the crowded café, past the waiters dressed in traditional black and white carrying silver platters of breakfast aloft, to the staff quarters, and then, I weave my way through the kitchens to the staircase that leads to the upper floors of the building.

Some of the kitchen staff look at me curiously, but I smile at them confidently, and they return to their tasks. These are strange times, and people are doing strange things.

Once I come to the back stairway, I start at the sight of Luciano waiting for me. My father works quietly, efficiently.

My admiration for him grows each day. As if by unspoken agreement, Luciano and I go upstairs together.

"Your father is extremely worried about you, and he has told me what you are doing today."

I nod, but my breathing becomes shallow as we walk toward the closed door that Luciano tells me houses Talia and Mario. My fingers curl around the note in the pocket of my coat. I have written out what I am doing today, so I can let Talia know without saying anything to Mario, without getting his hopes up or worrying him. Poor child. The circumstances under which he is living are deplorable.

I focus on the long hallway that is lined with sets of closed doors. We stop outside Talia and Mario's hiding place, and Luciano knocks a pattern on the door.

Talia opens the door, and at the sight of me, she pulls me into a hug.

"Nina! Luciano told me that you were interrogated." She looks across the room, where Mario is standing near the shuttered window, and after a glance up and down the hallway, she thanks Luciano, who melts away again, and she closes the door behind me.

"It seems ironic that it is you who are worried for my welfare," I say, my voice full of warmth. I hug her tightly again, holding her thin frame gently. "I am fine. It was nothing. Darling Talia, how are you?"

She wipes away a stray tear that falls onto her white cheek. "I'm living above the most illustrious café in Venice," she says, smiling now. "I remember begging my parents to bring me here, but they told me they could not afford it. That they did not have the money that the illustrious Orlandi family did."

Without mentioning where I am going, or whom I am trying to find today in order not to upset Mario, who is drawing quietly at a table now, I hand Talia the note I wrote in order to explain to her what I am doing, remove my coat, gloves, the olive-green skirt I am wearing, and the matching sweater. I take out a vivid red coat, and a black skirt and jumper. As quickly as possible, I don the light brown shingled wig, and take out my makeup pencil. I draw a round beauty spot above my right lip while Talia reads my note explaining that I am going to try to find Mario's parents.

"Are you going to a party?" Mario asks, suddenly, his small voice clear and unbearably innocent in this masquerade that I can't tell him about.

I force myself to chuckle, my fingers curling and uncurling in my pockets. "Oh, I wish I was going to a party, but no, I've just borrowed one of my mother's wigs for the festival today."

"Oh, my mama used to make her special almond cake because I wasn't allowed to cross the fun bridges over the Grand Canal for the festival. The cake was all lemony and fluffy!" He tilts his head to one side, a flush appearing on his cheeks, and my heart melts. "Do you think she'll make it again for me after the war?"

I move toward him, and gently tilt his chin upward toward me. "Of course I do," I say firmly.

When I turn to face Talia, her eyes are glistening, but she nods and busies herself with folding up laundry.

"Now, I must go, darling, but if I see any almond cake..." I try to make my eyes dance as best I can.

But Mario lowers his gaze to the ground. "Mama used to keep it warm for me, so it didn't go hard." His arms hang at his sides, slack, and his words are monotone.

Talia strokes his head and our eyes meet. Between us stands the little boy who is at the heart of all this.

I look at my watch. I must get going. I wish I could tell Mario that I'll bring him enough fluffy, lemony almond cake to feed him and all his friends, but I can't. I sniff, and pull a handkerchief from my pocket.

"Are you quite all right, Contessa?" Mario asks. "You are not crying?"

"No," I murmur, blowing my nose loudly at the open honesty of a child. "No, of course not," I say, with far more resolution than I feel.

"Signora," Luciano says, stepping out of the shadows at the end of the long hallway to accompany me back downstairs. He does not blink at my strange appearance. "There is something..." He reaches into his pocket and pulls out two folded pieces of paper. He presses them into my hand.

"Luciano," I breathe. I cannot believe it. "Where did you get these?"

He glances down the empty staircase that will lead me away from Talia's temporary sanctuary. A sanctuary that is surrounded by vipers who are searching for her, I remind myself, focusing on the fact that getting her away from the immediate vicinity where she is so well known and on the Nazis' wanted list is vital, as soon as I know whether or not Mario's parents are safe. "Your father."

I unfold the two *Kennkarten*, the Nazi identification papers that every citizen must carry in occupied territories. I know the Nazis would not be as "reasonable" as they were with me last time.

I am Julieta Marconi, and the woman in the photograph has features that are slightly blurred, but similar enough to mine to pass. Well done, Papa.

We start to move down the staircase. I pause briefly at the bottom. Above me, Talia and Mario await their fates, and it is up to me to do everything I can to ensure that things go in the right direction now. This is it.

Outside, the rain is falling in sheets. The sound of it pelting against the roof is like tiny bullets peppering the building. What

I must do is ensure that I merge in with the crowds. Of course, there are not as many people out due to the weather, but it provides a measure of obscurity.

"*Ciao*, Contessa," Luciano says.

"*Arrivederci*, Luciano."

I walk away from him, feeling like a stranger in my own city, and if it is that way for me, how must Talia be feeling?

I leave the Café Florian through the staff exit, and I risk stopping for a few seconds to scan the piazza. It is a sea of umbrellas that provide perfect coverage, and people are moving toward the Grand Canal. I cannot see Otto, and all I hope is that he cannot see me.

I put up my umbrella and walk into the thick of the crowd. The citizens are walking about quietly and patiently, probably too scared to draw attention to themselves given the sinister Nazi soldiers lining the edges of the square. All I must do is follow the route to Castello that I pored over last night, my map of Venice spread out on my bed.

For the first twenty-five minutes, everything goes like clockwork. The rain is steady but not torrential, until suddenly, it starts to fall as if it has been thrown out of a bucket. The shutters are closed on the old, pockmarked buildings. They are awash as if someone is hosing them down. I remind myself that I am grateful for the rain because there are no elderly men and women sitting on chairs, gossiping beneath their fluttering washing, no housewives queueing up for their rations at the local shops in the square, which are closed due to the sacred festival.

I just need to get across the piazza in front of me, and into the narrow street opposite. The square is almost flooded. Water is running ankle deep, and before long, I know it will be knee-high. I imagine that in the Piazza San Marco, workers are getting the makeshift walkways up quickly now.

I grip the handle of my black umbrella, now only feeling a slight twinge of pain after Wilhelm Moritz's meaty fingers pressed into mine, and march across the square in a determined clip.

I have only taken a few steps when it happens.

A figure emerges from the far side of the square.

CHAPTER 24

I stand for a moment, unable to move, staring openly across the square in Castello at the person who appears to have emerged from I do not know where. There are three other laneways running out of the piazza. In a split second, I must decide. I decide to take an alternative route, a diversion.

But as I turn and walk away, the figure approaches, walking toward me, clearly wanting me to stop. There is no shouting, and yet I propel myself away from them as quickly as possible, my heart pounding in my chest and my feet beating a pattern on the cobblestones. Their feet tap at the pavement too, sounding insistent, clipped, too close.

When they are alongside me, there is a lump in my throat the size of an orange, and yet I keep walking, trying not to look at them.

The person reaches out and grabs my arm.

"Signora," they say in Italian.

I almost fall down in a pool of relief, but I remind myself that Nazi could be speaking my language.

"Stop," the person says. I am listening to a woman's voice,

and she is clutching at my arm now. Knowing I have no choice, I turn to face my companion.

I am staring into the eyes of a woman around my age. Her hair is cut short in the style of a man, and she has strange amber eyes that lock with mine. She is dressed roughly, and in her hand, she is holding a small gun. I take in her ill-matched clothing, the streaks across her cheeks, the caked dirt on the hand that is pressed into my arm. If I am not mistaken, I am looking into the eyes of a partisan.

"I saw you approaching, signora," she says. "I know who you are."

Ten minutes later, I am sitting in a small apartment with the woman. A bare lightbulb swings from the cracked and peeling ceiling of the single room. The windows are boarded up and it is freezing in here, the only signs of habitation are four mattresses lined up on the floor. I shudder when I think of the cold comfort in the Nazis' offices at the Piazza San Marco. Here, while the partisans are fighting against the same enemy as I am, I feel only marginally less safe and secure.

A cupboard, bolted with a padlock sits above the makeshift beds. I shudder to think what they are storing in there, what their plans are, but then, in some strange way, I also admire their bravery, even though I hesitate to support the partisans' acts.

When the woman sits down opposite me, she takes her handgun out of her pocket, places it in her lap and regards me with her strange amber eyes. I'm only worried the gun will go off. I do hope she knows how to use it.

Quickly, I assess her appearance in order to distract myself from the weapon in her lap. She is dressed in an old pair of men's trousers, and her shirt looks like a man's too.

"Contessa Messina," she says, speaking evenly now. We

have already established that she knows my name, that Fedora and Lino Di Maggio informed her that I was Talia Baruch's friend.

I flick my gaze to the mattresses, and wrap my arms around myself.

She lifts her chin, her expression hardening. "Fedora and Lino told me to find you if anything happened to them, or if anything happens to Talia Baruch and the child is left alone."

I wait, Talia's name lingering between us, but just now, I want to keep quiet.

"I have never met Talia Baruch, but I know she was also working with the Di Maggios. That she was a close friend of theirs. And they told me that if anything happened to them, and to Talia, to find you." She pauses. "That you would take care of the child." The woman lowers her voice. "You come from one of the most prominent families in Venice. I have seen your photo in the newspaper society pages before the war. I knew who you were."

"I see."

"On the evening of the announcement in Verona, the Di Maggios were arrested by the Nazis."

I barely flinch, but my heart sinks like a rock to the bottom of a pond. Oh, poor Mario. I close my eyes to gather my thoughts. Of course they were arrested. It is the only explanation for the fact that they did not arrive at Talia's house to collect him that night.

"Were they going to take him out of Venice?" I ask.

The woman sends a quick glance across the room at the empty beds. "I don't know," she says, her voice monotone.

I shuffle my feet about under the table. My expensive boots feel ludicrous here. I can't help but think how impossible it is that darling little Mario is the child of these partisans, who left him with his teacher and put him at such risk. They knew Talia was also Jewish, that she would be in great danger.

I bite down my annoyance, and remind myself I'm thinking like my mother would.

"I saw them, being arrested right down in the piazza below the window," the woman says in her cold, monotone voice. "Ever since, I have kept a vigil up here, watching for Nazis." She shudders violently. "But, after it happened, I went to find Mario's mother to tell her that they were not here anymore... only to see you carrying the child out of the Baruchs' home. You already had him. And since then... I have not had any work to do." She looks down and fingers her gun for a moment.

I gasp. What is the woman implying? I don't allow myself to flinch. "But his mother had been taken."

The woman's eyes flash as she lifts her face again. "I was hoping you'd tell me she was alive." She gathers herself, continuing as my mind struggles to keep up with her, with what she is telling me, with what feels incomprehensible, but is starting to make real sense. "I went to get the child because his mother was likely to be arrested, and the Di Maggios were gone too," she says curtly. "I was going to bring him to your villa in Tuscany. The Di Maggios gave me your address, should their plan to collect the child from the Baruch's house go wrong."

My body is shaking now, fingers fumbling for each other, washing, washing my hands and finding no relief. "So the Di Maggios are Mario's adopted parents?" I ask, not wanting to sound like a fool. "And... Talia Baruch is Mario's birth mother?"

The woman leans her arms on the table. "Sì."

I picture the little boy, and relief washes over me because I found him, but this is tapered with anguish. I must protect him. And Talia has kept the fact that she is a mother from me for years?

CHAPTER 25

The old laneways of Castello merge into the *sestiere* of San Marco. Gone are the crumbling old buildings, the medieval alleys that have that centuries-old feel. Gone, too is everything I thought I knew about Talia. All I know is that she has kept a very big secret from me. And she never told me, not even in the last days, not even when I rescued her from the church. And I have no idea why.

But now, of course, it all makes perfect sense why she did not leave Venice with her father. She did not want to leave Mario alone in a war. Of course she didn't. My heart goes out to her for the awful choice she had to make, to say goodbye to her father, watch him depart Venice for a boat that would take him as a refugee across the Atlantic, alone, to America, an elderly gentleman with no family in a new country, while staying here with her son, with the little boy whom she couldn't bear to leave behind.

I place my hands over my face. What an awful choice.

But why, in six years, did she never tell me that she had a child of her own?

I stop, rain pattering on my umbrella, running in rivulets,

soaking the cobblestones, and polishing them so that they gleam. I glance around, but all I can hear is the soft patter of rain. Mercifully, it has lightened up a little in the last few minutes and is no longer falling in the deluge that felt like it was threatening to wash Venice away.

I move toward a nearby piazza. A group of teenagers are lingering under the shelter provided by a small portico to a lovely old church. The door is open, and I make my way toward it.

Inside, the altarpiece is beautiful. I feel that peaceful sense of hush that comes over me when I walk into any church in Venice. There is something magical about the churches here that I have not found anywhere else. It is the fact that we are surrounded by water, and the churches seem to be floating, giving them an even more unearthly feel. In the winter, they are especially inviting, with their candles and hushed atmosphere that seems to lend itself to the cold.

I pop a few lire in the wooden box by the candles, and light one for Mario. I go and sit right in the middle of the church. It is empty, save me. I sink down a moment, crossing myself and looking up at the Virgin Mary above the altar, the soft carpet that leads up the steps, the simple, beautiful frescoes that sit below the arched window. I pray for Talia, for her beloved father, wherever he is. And for her little boy.

And then, while I sit in the quiet of the church, I come up with a plan to get Talia and Mario out of Venice. The Nazis will not be nearly as skilled as a Venetian in navigating the unpredictable tides of the lagoon as I am. I know the shallows like the back of my hand. Venice was protected for centuries from invasion because only the Venetians knew how to enter, how to leave. Ships would simply get grounded. *Mimi* and I could lose a Nazi boat.

Then, I need to hand Talia and Mario to someone in the

resistance, someone who will guide her through Italy toward Spain and freedom.

The rain intensifies on the roof, and Nico's words ring through my mind as if in tune with the beating rain, and I clasp my hands tightly in my lap. When I get Talia out of Venice, will I ever see Jack again? An empty feeling forms in the pit of my stomach. I know that Jack would never come and settle down with me at the Villa Rosa. And deep down, I know that I could not leave the villa to be with him wherever he wants to live.

Friendship, my friendship with Talia will go on forever. Or so I hope. If I can get her and her beloved child out.

But my thoughts circle back to Jack, asking, what is this love that I have experienced with Jack? Love can be fleeting, I know that. The hard part is finding the strength to let go. For now, I have one big task to carry out for Talia. I must focus on that. And Jack? I just don't know.

Venice is a sea of gray all day. Gray merges with the rain, the sky, the water. There is a particular, muted beauty in its softness, and I go to the window back at my parents' palazzo and watch the slow procession of people crossing the makeshift bridges to the church of Santa Maria della Salute in the rain. I have never missed going to make my own visit to the old church before, and a part of me feels this is a bad omen, that I should be giving my thanks.

My mother's voice comes from behind me, where she is sitting reading a book on the sofa in the pink sitting room. "You have no idea how worried I am about you. This is not something you understand."

"I worry for both my boys every day. I most certainly understand what it is to be a mother."

I do not tell her that it is doubly difficult doing all the worrying on my own. Arturo had a way of talking to the boys that I lack. I have done my best since he died, but it has been a struggle, and I have certainly not done a perfect job.

I turn around and my mother taps her beautifully manicured fingers on the armrest. "I feel useless," she whispers. "Sitting here, while Europe burns."

I start and move across to sit opposite her. I search her face for signs of irony. But her wide eyes are sincere. "I never imagined that you felt this way." And she has never opened up to me like this before.

She glances at the door and lowers her voice. "I realize there is simply nothing I can do. It is an awful position to be in. And, yet, as a mother and a grandmother, my duty to my family must come first."

"But you could do something. You could help me."

She places her hands down on her open novel, and she looks up at me, and for the first time ever, I start talking openly and honestly to her.

"Tell me how you are feeling about the war now," I say to her. I need to establish where her loyalty lies, but my heart is beginning to swell with hope—a hope that I have never felt before when it comes to my mother.

"It is awful," she whispers. She looks down at her hands. "I never questioned who to follow before. My father always admired Mussolini. He was protective of people like us."

I wait.

"But a situation like this, the war, or a famine, like the one that happened centuries ago and inspired this festival today, it can alter your views. It can change you as a person, and I'm having nightmares. Nightmares about people like the Baruchs being taken away. I realize that I have been sheltered, wealthy. But I have not been able to see or have sympathy beyond this. I have lived in a cocoon of protection. Protected by the wealth of men. I'm only pleased that your father was able to get Talia and Doctor Baruch out of Venice. But there are others who have not been so lucky. Perhaps I should be doing something more to help."

"This is sudden," I can't help saying. And yet, my hands, which I spend so much time rubbing together that they are chafing, as well as pinching after being pressed so hard when I was questioned, are now trembling in my lap. A part of me wants to stand up, go to my mother and hug her. But still, there is a voice within me that tells me not to trust her. That this is some ruse.

She turns away, looking out the window at the sheets of rain. "There is something within me that wants to help. It is being locked away in this palazzo," she says. "Last night, I was sitting thinking about Nico, and his determination to make more money that this family does not need. Your father and I sat listening to him when he was here, and your father never questioned him. He never does."

"No, he adores you."

She stands up, moves toward the window, and leans heavily against the windowsill, her head resting on the windowpane almost connecting with the falling rain outside. "I know he does," she whispers. "That has been my security. My power, and my lack of agency all at once." She turns to me. "Do you understand?"

I sit and remember Arturo. She is right. Women have always held some sort of power if we are adored by men. There is almost a sense that this is our entire life, it applies to our status.

"And then there are the women who find their own strength," I say.

She turns to me. "I should have encouraged you to find your own strength. I know you were not in love with Arturo when you married him."

"You encouraged me into a relationship that is very like the one you have with my father. It worked. We fell in love. But when he died, I thought that my world had ended. I never want to feel that way again."

She comes back, and now she sits down next to me on the sofa. I cannot remember her ever doing this before. Coming to sit with me, coming to meet me.

"You know, I wanted so very hard to please you," I murmur. "I spent most of my life thinking I was never good enough. That I never meet your standards."

"You are enough," she says to me. She reaches out, as if to take my hands. And then she stops, her beautiful face creasing up into a frown. "Your hands look sore," she whispers, gently holding them for the first time I can ever remember. "Let me give you something soothing to rub on them, my daughter. And let me help you, with whatever it is that is troubling you. Is it something to do with Jack?"

She is still holding my hands, her touch impossibly gentle.

I look away, and slowly, I shake my head. "I need to save Talia and her son, and I am terrified we won't make it."

She is quiet.

Quickly, trusting her for the first time in my life with the truth, I tell her about Talia and Mario... as much as I know.

She is unflinching, simply nodding, holding my hand.

"I have her and Mario in hiding. I am going to take them out of Venice in *Mimi*. From there, I plan to take them to Ravenna, where I need to place her into the hands of the partisans, so that she can get away. Because I don't know where her home will ever be safe to her again."

"No, she should stay with family. She is as close as family after all. My sister, Gabriella, will help her." My mother leans forward and brushes a stray strand of my hair away from her face. "I will contact her." She looks away. "I haven't spoken to her in years, but I know whose side she will be on. And it is time that I joined the right side too."

"Thank you," I say, softly. "It is important for families to stick together."

"And it is important for women to stick together too. Poor Talia," she says. "I wonder what happened to the child's father."

"I have no idea, who he was or is, Mama." But I feel all the tension that I've bottled up inside myself for decades about my mother fall away in a big release. Finally, I feel as if I can talk openly with her.

That night, I sit up and try to put everything together. I have myself, my boat, an offer of assistance from my mother, and I need to have a plan. My father told me quite reasonably this afternoon that I would be better to leave Talia above the Café Florian, that Luciano would look after her and she would be safe there.

But the Germans are putting up a great resistance to the Allies' efforts to move up through Italy. When the Allied armies finally arrive in Rome, it is going to be a bloodbath, and it is going to be months, even years, before they come to Venice and who knows how much longer this war will go on. What is more, the world is surely more focused on what is going on in France. The stories that are coming out of there are horrendous, and they have been living under the Nazis since 1940, so I do not begrudge them the fact that an Allied invasion to liberate that country must be a priority. I fear it will be a long time before the Allies send enough troops to properly liberate Italy.

But the resistance network in Italy is growing. It is not only the partisans hiding out in the hills or the anarchists and the communists in the cities hiding away with guns and waiting for the Allies to arrive that are working here. It is not only the priests and the nuns in the churches. There is a network. And this network is simply made up of friends. One friend reaches out to another, we help each other, and that is how this is going to work. I never anticipated that one of those friends might be my mother.

CHAPTER 26

A plan is starting to form. My mother has contacted her sister in Ravenna, and she has offered to hide Talia and Mario. What's more, my aunt is aware of the resistance network in her city and is going to reach out to them and establish how we can move Talia and Mario safely through Italy so that she and Mario can escape. Like so many other refugees, they will have to go on foot. But I am beginning to see that they will not be alone.

The following morning, the *acqua alta* is still at knee height, but the rain has stopped, and I have made my way across the temporary walkways that crisscross the Piazza San Marco to the cathedral, where I have lit a candle for Mario.

I go to a pew, allowing the comfort of the golden mosaics to soothe me. I bow my head, praying for both of my sons. Wishing they were with me, hoping that one day we will be together again. It worries me that I have not had a letter from Raf in months. I look down at my hands, gently clasped, rather than being rubbed over and over, the liniment that my mother gave me yesterday already starting to soothe the redness that they bear.

I pray that I will be a better mother—no, a different mother than I have been so far. I wince now at the fact that I interfered in Raf's life before he left for the war. I know that he has feelings for my secretary Cara, and I warned him off, forbade him from having a relationship with her.

I press my palms to my forehead. The last thing I wanted to be was like my mother. Now, I only hope that I can get through to my children before it is too late, that I find the courage to be more like my mother is being now. This is a huge change for me.

When someone slips in beside me in the pew, I start. Slowly, I turn to him. I would know him anywhere.

Without turning to me, he reaches into his pocket, and slips a piece of paper into my hand. I know what it is without looking. A *Kennkarte*. False papers for Talia.

Jack reaches out and squeezes my hand. "How are you?" he whispers.

"Perfectly fine. And you?"

He sighs. "*Si*, Lina. I cannot complain."

I take in a sharp breath. A priest is walking up the aisle toward us, slowly. I only exhale when he passes by. I can't help but remember all my visits to the churches in Venice, how some priests and nuns were not supportive of the Jews. I hate to say it, but I do not know who is reporting whom at this point.

"You know of Gino Amato?" Jack whispers.

I frown. "Of course, the cyclist." Gino Amato is a celebrity in Italy. He is a famous cyclist who rides in the Tour de France.

"He is riding around Italy and touring the cities to lift people's spirits," Jack says. He glances along the empty pew. The priest stops at the back of the church and engages in a whispered conversation with another member of the clergy. "But he is also creating a distraction, so that resistance workers can get refugees out of those cities, while crowds gather in the squares to see him."

I do not move.

"He is coming to Venice. I can contact him and ask him to

appear in San Marco Square while you take Talia and Mario out of Venice."

I think of Jack's crystal radio set hidden away in his bedroom and shudder. Six weeks. Six weeks is the length of time that radio operators in France are given to live. Jack is taking huge risks, but I need to get this moving. The longer I put off moving Talia, the more danger everyone will be in.

Slowly, I nod my head.

I make concrete plans. I contact an old friend, Giuseppe Parella, the fishmonger, and arrange for him to deliver a crate of fish to the Café Florian. I will spirit Talia and Mario downstairs, and Giuseppe will swap the fish for Talia and Mario, placing them in the crate. I will leave the café with a crate containing two people, supposedly fish, which I will have purchased from Giuseppe as a gift for my cousin who lives in Ravenna.

I will meet my cousin out in the far reaches of the lagoon.

From there, Jack has planned by code with his American contacts to get Talia and the children out of Ravenna as stow-aways on a troopship full of injured GIs.

And Gino Amato will provide distraction and entertain-ment in San Marco Square for the crowds who will convolute the area for us.

I will go into the Café Florian at precisely ten o'clock after going into San Marco Cathedral as I often do, where I will meet Papa for coffee, and then I shall go upstairs and collect Mario and Talia once we can see that Otto Ablenz is suitably distracted by the famous cyclist. Talia knows of the plan because my father has relayed it to Luciano who has informed her that we will be getting her to safety, out of Venice, away from Europe, to America. She will be ready and waiting along with Mario.

We must hope that, this time, nothing goes wrong, no one

changes their minds, and that Mario and Talia can live freely not only for the remainder of this war, and who knows how long it will continue, but for the rest of their lives.

The night before I am due to take them to safety, I cannot sleep. I pace around my bedroom and make the mistake of listening to the illicit BBC news. The British are reporting that all the Jews in the ghettos in Italy have been forcibly removed to the camps. Their reporters, just like Jack, are stationed in occupied territories, but not in Germany, as it is considered too dangerous.

Since the convention of Verona, it is now estimated that not hundreds, but thousands of Italian Jews have been transferred in cattle trucks to a camp in Poland, which is fast garnering the reputation as the worst prison camp in the Third Reich. Stories are really starting to evolve of trains with long, snaking carriages arriving daily at this camp, of Jewish children, the elderly, forced into freezing conditions with winter coming on, with no lavatory facilities, no food, no water.

The reporter launches into the story of a boy whose mother was rounded up in the Jewish ghetto in Rome. Seeing her being placed in the back of a cattle truck, the child went out screaming into the street, only to be arrested on the spot. He was thrown in the back of the truck with her. When the truck stopped at a traffic light, his mother took advantage of the situation and pushed him out into the street. The boy immediately ran to the tram stop and boarded the bus. The ticket collectors and drivers allowed him to ride the bus until a passenger recognized him and reunited him with his father.

The reporter said that this woman had given this boy life, twice. Once when he was born, and once when she saved him from the prison camps.

The BBC went on to say that their source in Italy confirmed that he will most likely never see his mother again.

Even though we have not seen any pictures in our Nazi-controlled newspapers that reflect the stories that are coming from the BBC, the risk that Talia and I are taking tomorrow feels heavy as lead. But the alternative, leaving her and Mario here is even more unpalatable.

I am washed and dressed well before dawn breaks. And as soon as the first glimmer of pink light shines on the edge of my black curtains, I scurry downstairs and make myself a pot of strong coffee.

Precisely on time, I stand at the entrance to the Piazza San Marco, not far from the place where I was intercepted by the Nazis and questioned by Wilhelm Moritz and Otto Ablenz. I struggle to use their names, because it feels like humanizing them, but in doing so, it alleviates my fear of them. It helps, because otherwise I would view them as nameless monsters.

I am acutely aware that Otto Ablenz is a few steps behind me. If I turn around and come face to face with him, I worry that I will lose my nerve.

The *acqua alta* has receded, but now the Piazza San Marco is covered in a layer of sludge. I make my way across it, threading along the wooden walkways.

Workers are already in attendance cleaning up the mess. Nazis watch them in groups.

I hurry over to the San Marco Cathedral. Inside, a choir of elderly monks is singing Gregorian chants. I sink down into one of the pews and let the music soak through me.

I kneel and pray for Talia and her son.

Finally, I stand up, a little soothed by the soaring, yet delicate golden beauty of Venice's cathedral. I light a candle on the way out for her.

Outside, I spot Otto already seated at a table outside Café Florian. He is ostensibly reading a newspaper, but he looks up as I approach keeping my gaze steadfastly away from him, walking with pride.

I step inside the warmth of Café Florian, and nearly all the clientele is in Nazi uniform.

I hear the tinkle of a young woman's laughter. She is blond, with her hair combed back and her curls waving softly around her shoulders. I do not know whether she is German or Italian, but she is enjoying the full spread of morning tea with a handsome Nazi soldier.

Luciano materializes next to me, and I see the way he shoots a glance out to where Otto is sitting. One of his waiters is serving coffee to the Nazi, and while Otto is occupied, Luciano neatly leads me out of sight from the window and takes me to the private booth we have booked for my breakfast with Papa.

Papa is sitting under a fresco of exquisitely dressed women at a picnic in the countryside. The moment he sees me, he stands up and kisses me on both cheeks. I try to smile bravely at the ashen color of his cheeks, at the redness of his eyes, at the way they dart back and forth over my face, and inside, my feelings mirror his.

A waiter brings us coffee and a plate of morning tea.

I start when a waiter drops a teacup somewhere in the café. Agitated, I shift about in my seat, unable to stop peering around and seeing whether Otto is watching me. He is there.

I glance at my watch, dig in my purse to keep my hands occupied. As if understanding my anguish, Papa reaches out and catches my other hand. In precisely twenty minutes, Gino Amato will appear in the square, and in twenty-five minutes, Giuseppe will arrive with his catch of fish, which will be scaled, filleted and ready for Sunday luncheon service at the Café Florian. He will arrive precisely at the time when the Nazi who is stationed at the trade entrance to the café will be on his fifteen-minute coffee break. I have given myself ten minutes to get Talia and Mario out of the room upstairs, down into the fish crate, and out into *Mimi* whom I have parked in the dock as I have for the last two mornings in order not to create any questions in Otto's head.

The local news reported faithfully that Gino Amato was coming to Venice this morning, with a Nazi addendum stating that things were just as they should be under the Reich, and that Amato was a good citizen who would be riding to represent Germany in the future. I listened to this while I clipped the earrings that my late husband gave me on our last wedding anniversary into my ears. "Dearest Arturo," I whispered to him. "Watch over us all today."

The young cyclist will station himself in clear view of Otto Ablenz, while Luciano will instruct one of his waiters to suggest that Otto's coffee is kept warm so that he can walk across the square and hear Gino Amato speak.

Jack has established that in Otto's spare time, he loves to watch sports.

Now, Luciano appears in my line of sight. At precisely the right time, he stands among the other bustling waiters and nods at me.

Otto has moved.

I stand up, my heart pounding in my mouth. I allow my gaze to dart down to Papa, but he is staring down at his untouched plate of food, his lips pale.

Luciano and I rush past each other, and I take the false identity papers that are folded in his palm as he does so and place them in my pocket.

My heart palpitating, and my hands shaking, I take the back stairs up to the floor where Talia is hiding with Mario. She is sitting on her bed with the child next to her. They are holding hands.

A well of emotion courses through me. It seems like an age since I found Mario hidden in the laundry chute. And it seems like another lifetime when I first met my darling friend.

Talia stands up and comes to me. Our hug is long and heart-felt and I pull Mario in toward me too. Luciano's messages to her have been clear and she is ready. We move toward the door. I look at my watch. The Nazi on duty at the water entrance to the Café Florian will be going on his break now.

We walk downstairs in silence as I promised Luciano. The kitchen is cleared of staff as he promised. No one is to witness this. The only person standing with his trolley and three empty boxes by the tradesmen's door is my old fisher friend, Giuseppe, who has long supplied my father with spoils from the sea.

The middle-aged man with his stubbled chin tips his fisher-man's cap toward me, but he glances worriedly toward Talia.

And then, I am standing opposite Talia. "I will take care of you both," I whisper.

Her arms wrap around me, and I breathe in deeply, my face pressed into her soft dark curls.

"Thank you, Nina," she says simply. My childhood nick-name feels like a protective shawl wrapping around us. Surely, everything will be all right.

I nod firmly through my tears, repeatedly, and she turns and climbs into the box. Giuseppe hands Mario to her and he climbs in with no questions asked.

The last thing I see before their crate is closed is her face turned up toward Giuseppe, thanking him too.

Giuseppe rests a hand on my shoulder for a moment. "Well done, Evie," he says.

The tears fall down my face freely now, my lip is wobbling, and my nose is tingling unbearably. The tension that I felt last night is coming out of me in a big release.

I tighten the belt of my coat as Giuseppe loads the crates onto a trolley and wheels my best friend out through the back kitchen door to the landing stage.

CHAPTER 27

Finally, I steer *Mimi* away from the Grand Canal, and out into the Venetian lagoon. I keep my eyes trained straight ahead as Venice recedes behind us. Carefully, I navigate the deeper sections of the lagoon, noticing where the fishing boats are traveling, the boats that belong to the most recent generations of fishermen who have lived on the outer islands since Venice materialized.

A cold breeze stirs out here, and it is quiet, too quiet. I shall meet my cousin at the entrance to the Gulf of Venice, where the lagoon ends, and widens out into the open sea. It is a little rough, and *Mimi* bounces up and down on the wavelets. I only hope Talia and Mario are not feeling seasick. I wish I knew.

When my cousin's boat comes into view, I tap the box where Talia and Mario are hiding. Glancing about carefully, I check that there are no Nazi boats in sight.

But everything is clear.

My cousin's boat moves steadily toward us. This is it. We have no time to say goodbye properly, but I take a tiny risk and open the lid of the crate.

Talia looks up at me, Mario's face buried in her chest. And I can see it, the back of his head, shaped like hers, the mass of curls. She is his mother.

"I wish you'd told me," I murmur. "Does he know?" I say.

She tips her head back, her hand running over Mario's tousled head. "I told no one," she murmurs. "Except him." She drops a kiss on Mario's head, and he nestles in closer to her. "The Di Maggios formally adopted Mario when he was a baby, because they understood. They knew how I would be treated as an unmarried mother, and a Jew."

I bring a shaky hand to my forehead, forcing my eyes away from the crate that is affording them such cramped safety for a short while.

My cousin's boat draws closer, and I to them.

"Not your father?" I ask.

"No. I went to Switzerland for a year when I was pregnant," she says, whispering softly.

"And the father?" I ask, my voice croaking.

"A short affair," she says.

I sigh. "I see. I wish you'd—"

"It was the year after you lost Arturo," she says, her voice mingling with the breeze, carrying with the sea birds who swoop and dive over the silent Venetian lagoon. Out there is the open sea, the place beyond this ancient protected city that was our home, until recently. Whether Venice will ever be Talia's home again is something I don't know. I dare not hope. I dare not hope for a better world, a world without this war, a world where I can live openly side by side with my best friend and her young son.

I stay quiet, steering *Mimi*. "You still could have told me. There was no shame."

"I went to Switzerland for the last five months of the pregnancy, and Fedora and Lino and I were already working together, but they couldn't have a child." She stares up at me from the confines of the crate, her eyes glassy.

"I am praying for them," I whisper.

"And so am I," she murmurs. "The father... my friend, wanted to marry me."

My hands still, my leather gloves pinching my fingers and a wave of heat passes over me. "Whatever went wrong?" I murmur. If she had a husband, this might have all turned out so differently. She could have left Venice safely with her father and her husband.

Annoyance washes over me. If he left her, with child and alone, then that is awful.

But she reaches up with her free hand, one hand still stroking Mario's head. "He wanted to marry me and turn me into a good Jewish wife," she whispers, her eyes, hollow and worried, light up with a little of that delicious Talia spark that I saw that very first day. "I would have had to give up everything —my teaching, the children I loved working with, my independence... and my child would have grown up as the natural Jewish child of an unmarried woman. It was too dangerous for Mario even when there was only talk of a Nazi war."

The other boat draws up close to us. My hands turn numb, my body cold, and I feel a hysterical desire to turn around with *Mimi* and Talia and Mario and take them back to the villa with me. But I know it's no good. I can't protect them, and we need to get them out of Italy now. It is too dangerous here, in our own country, for either of them to stay.

"I understand," I whisper. "But, darling, you must know that you can tell me anything..."

"You had your own grief." And our eyes lock for the last time that day, and for the first time in my life, I see the slight wrinkles around her stunning brown eyes, the knowledge and understanding that comes from being a middle-aged woman.

"Yes," I concede, "But I would have always helped my dearest friend."

I take a good look around to check the lagoon is clear. A

flight of birds takes off from one of the islands that surrounds Venice. And in the far distance, I can see the shape of San Marco Cathedral, my home beacon, and it comforts me.

My cousin pulls up quietly next to us, and quickly, I lift Mario out of the crate, hold his little body close to mine a moment, "God bless you," I whisper into his hair. "Sweet child, may God keep you safe," and he presses my hand.

"I'll be fine," he says bravely. "I will take care of my mama."

He is in the arms of my cousin, and I help Talia out of the crate.

We stand opposite each other. "*Arrivederci*," I barely manage.

"My dearest friend," she says.

And then my cousin helps her climb aboard his boat, and he starts up the engine.

I stand alone on *Mimi's* deck, watching the boat as it draws away into the distance, and when it's time to turn around and go back to Venice, I let out an uncontrollable sob.

That night, I sit in Elisabetta's living room with her and Jack. Elisabetta and I cooked risotto with pumpkin. We laughed and sang old songs as we cut vegetables together. Jack and I have been stepping around each other politely all evening. We have both joined in Elisabetta's elation at the outcome for Talia and the little boy whom we have all grown fond of, but there is a strange sense of anticlimax at the same time. And neither Jack nor I have acknowledged the question that is lingering in the air between us, unspoken.

What next?

I have my feet tucked up under me on the sofa.

Elisabetta waved my question away kindly when I asked her if she would mind very much if I removed my shoes and sat in my stockinged feet.

"Dearest Evelina, you have the right to spend the rest of your life in your stockings if you so wish," she said.

Now, she stands up and yawns.

"It is time for me to rest now, my young ones," she says.

Jack laughs, and almost snorts. I chuckle alongside him.

"Goodnight, Nonna," Jack murmurs.

She rests a hand on his shoulder. "You have both done well," she says. "Please, get some rest, won't you."

"Thank you," I say to Elisabetta, meaning it. "It was such fun to cook with you tonight."

"It is always a pleasure to see you, my dear." She smiles at me, and she disappears through the room into her bedroom wing.

"Whiskey? Port wine?" Jack asks.

I shake my head. The alertness that overtook me earlier has dissolved into a valley of tiredness. Despite having slept fitfully this afternoon, I feel a strange sense of emptiness and exhaustion. Perhaps it is because my job is done. There is no reason for me to stay in Venice, and it is this that leaves me feeling strange and empty.

Jack walks over to the drinks cabinet, as any middle-aged man might while his wife rested on the sofa. He pours himself a small shot of whiskey, pads back over to the sofa, sits down, regards me. "You asked me a question before, and I did not answer it."

I raise my eyes to look at him. "Yes?" I say softly.

"I want to spend the rest of my life with you."

"You told me that once before." I eye him, but take a deep breath to slow my racing heartbeat.

"I know," he whispers.

"Are you going to walk out on me again?"

"No," he says. "Never. And I'm sorry I left without fighting, and I'm sorry we missed all the years we could have had together, my darling. But I love you, and I want to spend the rest of my life with you, and I want to leave no stone unturned to make this work."

"But I live in a villa in Tuscany, and you, you roam the world. I'd need you to show up for me, if this was to work," I say. *And no, I'm not that girl who'd travel to New York for you anymore*, I don't add. *I have a life that I love, that I don't want to give up.*

"I think I could learn to make a good olive oil." His eyes hold that fire that drew me in from the moment I met him back in the ballroom of the Hotel Excelsior. "And if there's a story to write, I'll write it, but I'll always stay with you."

And I'm nineteen, and I'm in his arms, and we're slow dancing, but the thing is, I know now that I'm also an independent woman of forty-three.

"I love you too, Jack," I whisper, and gently, he caresses my cheek with the side of his hand, and he leans down, and draws me up from the sofa, and he kisses me.

I'm still in his arms when there is a deafening thump on the front door.

We freeze for what feels like a long moment but is only a second.

And then, we both stare at each other in alarm as the sound of German voices ricochets into the stairwell outside the apartment.

Boots pound up the marble stairs to Elisabetta's home; they must have broken the entire front door to the palazzo down. In three seconds flat, they are banging on Elisabetta's door, and yelling. Their words are incomprehensible.

It sounds like there is a whole group of them. Automatically, Jack and I come even closer together, hugging each other for what must be the shortest time imaginable, and yet it feels like forever, as if I am at home and I do not want to let go, that if I stay here, in his arms, all will be well.

The thumping continues. They start kicking the door.

Jack holds my shoulders and looks straight into my eyes. "Go down the hallway to the laundry. Get in the laundry chute."

"No, Jack, I will stay with you. We have only just found our way back to each other. I'm not leaving you now."

He pulls me to him again, frantically stroking my hair. "When you get in the laundry chute, ease your way down to the ground floor. It will be a soft landing. There are clothes at the bottom."

I am shaking. My teeth are chattering. It sounds like they are hitting the door with bayonets. It will not be long now, not long...

"Run, darling," he whispers. His voice is lost in the havoc outside in the hallway, and I know that I will always remember the feeling of him standing, helplessly, there.

"Not without you," I whisper, but he is already moving toward the bedroom wing. As I rush to the hallway door, I see the flash of his pistol.

I bump into Elisabetta outside her bedroom. She is in her nightgown, her eyes wild. *"Jack?"* she asks.

I let out a sob and clutch her.

"Come with me," I beg her.

"No, Evelina," she whispers. "They know I live here. They are not after me. They are after you. Go, now. Please. Do as Jack says."

I search her face, but she gives me a little push.

I run down the hallway to the laundry, my hands fumble on the door, and I open cupboards until I find the laundry chute. In a flash, I am inside, and I jump.

Once I am down on the ground floor, safe in the padding of Elisabetta's washing, I crane my head, my ear against the corresponding door downstairs, straining to listen out for any telltale signs that they have left a watch party downstairs. I need not have bothered. A few moments later, I am assailed with a sound that I know will haunt me for the rest of my life. Elisabetta is wailing. Jack's muffled curses shiver in the air next to her. I sit, my head buried in my hands.

They are taking her out in her dressing gown. What sort of people do not care that a woman is over eighty? That she has not hurt anyone in her whole life?

My entire body starts to tremble uncontrollably.

I hear Jack, bless him, telling them off, shouting at them. There is the sound of a scuffle. Still, Jack yells at them to spare his grandmother.

But then I hear the sneer of Otto Ablenz's voice.

The sound of someone slipping and tumbling on the stairwell. Elisabetta's scream. Them rough-handling Jack and his grandmother. And then the front door to the palazzo slams, and through the thick walls, I can hear nothing out in the street.

I do not waste any time. I run back upstairs to Elisabetta's flat. Grab the key that Elisabetta keeps on the table by the front door, lock it. I can try at least to keep her home safe.

I go out into the cold, Venetian night. The Nazis, Jack and Elisabetta have disappeared. They will have loaded them into a boat heading into the wintry night.

I slip home through the darkness like some wild urchin. Hiding in alleyways, turning corners at the hint of any footsteps within earshot.

The palazzo is silent when I arrive. My parents are both sleeping, and I decide not to wake them. Instead, I sit up, sporadically closing my eyes, fall into a nightmare-fueled sleep. Every time I wake, I try to placate myself that Elisabetta and Jack have only been taken in for questioning. But in my distressed state, I cannot stop the dreadful sense of horror that curls through me. They were taken away because of me.

. . .

When dawn comes, I wake up, curled up in a ball on the sofa.

I grab my coat, throw it on, and walk out the front door.

In fifteen minutes, I am knocking on the door of Wilhelm Moritz's office. I will argue this man to the death if I must. I will not let them take Elisabetta and Jack away. We have fought too hard, come this far, sacrificed too much. The Nazis have done enough, and the strong contessa in me will not stand for anymore.

The blond woman I saw at the Café Florian yesterday answers the door and ushers me in. I was not afforded the greeting of a receptionist when I last visited here.

She sits me in the anteroom to one of the old offices of the Venetian council. The floor is parquet, there is the smell of coffee, the scent of her expensive perfume.

Chanel, I force myself to think.

My breath is ragged. I fold my hands on my lap stubbornly and wait.

"I wish to see him immediately," I say, after half an hour.

She disappears in through Moritz's door.

"Enter," she tells me. It is a command, not an invitation.

I stand up, fold my arms, and walk toward the door.

Inside, Wilhelm Moritz is sitting in a cloud of smoke.

"Sit down, Contessa," he says expansively.

"You have arrested two innocent people," I say, remaining standing. My voice is surprisingly clear. And, buoyed by this, I hold his gaze.

"I think we have not," he says.

"Where are they?"

He folds his arms and sits back in his seat. He raises his cigar to his lips and blows out a wave of fresh fumes. "Let me answer your first point initially," he says, in clipped, painful Italian. "Our informer was well respected, and, let me say, perfectly clear."

I wait.

He sits back and crosses his legs. "He lives in Milano. You might know him. His name is Nicolas Messina." He looks at me.

Nico. No, I thought you understood. In that moment, my heart breaks once more. *Not my son.*

"He was forthright in telling us that Jack Sabo has been sending coded reports, classified information back to the United States, rather than reporting the truth, as per our agreement with him. We were suspicious, but your son tells us that he overheard you speaking about it with the journalist and... praising him for his valor. His craftiness." Moritz sounds like he is relishing his own words.

"You are lying."

"Oh no, my dear. Quite the opposite." He pushes a piece of paper across the desk, and I notice that his hands are fleshy and pink, his fingernails slightly too long.

I look at the paper, but I do not touch it.

It is a written statement in what is undoubtedly my son's handwriting. Nico's was always immaculate. Raf's is always a mess. I am unable to stifle my sob as I remember Nico sitting down and helping his younger brother, while Raf clutched his pen in his fist, his tongue sticking out as he concentrated so hard.

Bile courses up through my throat. *My son, what have you done?*

"The traitorous journalist has a grandmother who has been harboring him. Blatantly breaking the rules that we made clear on our arrival in Venice two months ago. Everyone was warned. This was her choice."

He pulls out a drawer in his desk and takes out Jack's crystal

radio set. They must have been back to the apartment, in spite
of my efforts. I curse myself for not thinking about it.

I do not even look at it. I refuse to acknowledge it. Instead, I
hold Wilhelm's gaze. "Where are they, Herr Moritz?"

"On a first-class train to Poland. We did not wish to any to
take any chances and so commenced the journey before the
break of dawn." He inspects his watch matter-of-factly. "Yes,
they are well out of Italy by now."

I curl my hands into fists. Again, that wave of loss that I felt
when saying goodbye to Talia almost knocks me backwards,
threatens to flatten me.

I stare at him in horror. And the room starts to swim. I am in
a nightmare. I dig my nails into the palms of my hands in the
hope that I will wake up. I blink a few times, but all I hear is the
delighted sound of Wilhelm's laughter. It is rich and deep, and
it sears into my heart, into my bones. I want it out. I want him
away. I want Jack and Elisabetta back.

Jack's face flashes before me. The night we first met, the
way he came over and asked me in that New York accent of his
whether I would like to dance.

He has not been doing anything wrong. The dear man has
been helping the Allied cause, trying to fight against hope in a
world that has gone insane.

I have heard too much about those cattle trains. It is
unlikely that Elisabetta will even survive the journey.

Somehow, I move toward the office door.

Then, at the last moment I turn around and face Wilhelm.

The smoke has cleared. And I see him clearly now. He is a
little man, a little middle-aged man.

Despair and horror wash over me. I could not save Jack and
Elisabetta, but possibly, in their final act, they saved me. While
my son, my own flesh and blood, is ultimately to blame.

CHAPTER 28

THE VILLA ROSA, 1948

I am sitting on the terrace outside the Villa Rosa. It is summer and in front of me, Cara has placed a dish of olives, local honey, focaccia scattered with rosemary, and soft French cheese.

It is almost five years since Jack was sent to Auschwitz concentration camp in Poland. Since the war, tales of the atrocities have shocked the world, but they had little chance of survival. Elisabetta was shot on arrival, suffering and weak after the long journey in the unspeakable train. At the end of the war, I learned that Jack died just before the liberation of the camp.

There is not a day that goes by when I do not think of them. There is not a day that goes by when my heart does not break. I continue living each day, but without my best friend and the man I love, life has never felt the same. My parents are safely in their palazzo on the Grand Canal, and their lives continue along with the ebb and flow of the water that runs in front of their home, but I know by the haunted expression in their eyes whenever they see me, I know when they look at me and don't mention Nico anymore, when they avoid any talk of the war, that they have come to an understanding of the extent of the tragedy that played out for Jack, and how deeply that has broken my heart.

It is difficult for me to focus a few minutes later, when I see a figure coming up the driveway. Every time someone comes to see me, my heart races and I imagine Jack, my darling son Rafael, or maybe, even Nico for he is still my son... and my emotions are a mess. When it comes to Nico, I have struggled. Being betrayed by my own son left me in a state of shock and horror, and for a long time, I simply shut people out. In the end, Nico couldn't bear for me to live my own life. I know that his actions had far-reaching consequences, and while for a long time after the war, I felt I had failed as a mother, I now also understand that as an adult, he made his own decisions, and his choices were something I could do nothing about.

Since those awful, tumultuous years, I have also worked hard to try to track down Esther, the friend of Talia's that I met in the holding prison at Giudecca, but to no avail. She never came home.

But now, someone is walking up the driveway. No, not one person... two. I stand up, and from up here on the terrace, I can make out the two figures coming from the entrance gate below the lowest part of the garden. As they come into focus, my hands fly to my necklace, one that Arturo gave me.

I give out a little cry, and stuttering, stammering, my lips moving now and nothing coming out, I run down the driveway like a schoolgirl.

"Talia?" My voice is shaky, soft, halting.

But she is here and she throws herself into my arms. And I hold her, and then, beside her, I see a young man who is far taller than he was six years ago, and he has sparkling brown eyes and a tousle of hair and he smiles at me, and there's a dimple in his right cheek.

"Contessa?" he asks, tentatively.

"Mario," I say, one hand still lingering in Talia's. She looks well, and healthy and her eyes are bright. But even as I hold her son, I notice the way she is looking around.

"Where is Jack?" she asks.

And I shake my head. "Jack was betrayed and sent to Poland... he was reported to the Nazis by my own son, by Nico," I whisper, drawing my cardigan around my body. "I've tried to accept that my son is an adult who makes his own decisions, but, oh Talia... I felt the most awful sense of failure for a long time."

"I'm so sorry, darling Nina. There are not words." She bows her head for a few moments, and we are quiet, remembering Jack. "I know you loved Jack. I loved him as a friend too."

She speaks haltingly at first, but then her words grow in conviction. "But you *are* a wonderful friend and a good mother. You have given me everything." Her brown eyes meet mine, and she reaches up and tucks a stray dark curl behind her ear. Her hair, her skin is healthy again, and slowly, despite the tragedy of losing our darling friend Jack, she reaches out her hand and enfolds my hands in hers. "I am back now, Nina. And that is because of you."

"And Contessa, I feel like I've got two mothers," Mario says, looking up at me. "Thank you."

I lean down and take his face in my hands, this child who, somehow, represents everything. Everything that I have tried to do in my life. Yes, he represents that time of incredible difficulty and loss in Venice, but at the same time, when I look at him, I feel hope. I feel that it is time to move forward from the past.

A LETTER FROM ELLA CAREY

Dear reader,

I want to say a huge thank you for choosing to read *The Venetian Daughter*. If you did enjoy it and want to keep up to date with all my latest releases, just sign up at the following link. Your email address will never be shared, and you can unsubscribe at any time.

www.bookouture.com/ella-carey

I hope you loved *The Venetian Daughter* and if you did, I would be very grateful if you could write a review. I'd love to hear what you think, and it makes such a difference helping new readers to discover one of my books for the first time.

I love hearing from my readers—you can get in touch through social media or my website.

Thanks,

Ella x

www.ellacarey.com

facebook.com/ellacareyauthor
x.com/Ella_Carey

ACKNOWLEDGMENTS

Thank you to the entire team at Bookouture for their work on this novel, especially to my editor Maisie Lawrence, copyeditor Jade Craddock, proofreader Anne O'Brien, the cover designer, Sarah Whittaker, the marketing team, and thanks to Sarah Hardy for her work on the publicity for the book. Huge thanks to my family, friends, to my readers and to the bloggers who so kindly read and write about my books. I am enormously appreciative of your support.

PUBLISHING TEAM

Turning a manuscript into a book requires the efforts of many people. The publishing team at Bookouture would like to acknowledge everyone who contributed to this publication.

Audio
Alba Proko
Sinead O'Connor
Melissa Tran

Commercial
Lauren Morrissette
Hannah Richmond
Imogen Allport

Cover design
Sarah Whittaker

Data and analysis
Mark Alder
Mohamed Bussuri

Editorial
Maisie Lawrence
Ria Clare

Made in the USA
Coppell, TX
25 September 2024